BJ

## Stolen Horses

When young wrangler Quince Simms lands a job tending the sixty-horse remuda of Big John Durham on his south Texas spread he's well pleased. It's hard work but it's honest. The trouble is that he's fallen for the charms of the rancher's daughter, Marie, and when his boyhood pal, the leather-clad, fast-shooting dude, Lance Silverlight arrives on the scene, it's a recipe for disaster!

Not only does the handsome Lance sweet-talk Marie into the hay, but he also heads for the border taking the rancher's remuda with him. Now it's up to Quince to strap on his Colt and cross the Rio Grande in pursuit of the stolen horses. Can the lone youngster outshoot Silverlight and take his former friend back for his hanging?

And will Marie thank him?

*By the same author*

Black Pete – Outlaw
The Last of the Quantrill Riders
Duel at Silverillo
Death at Sombrero Rock
The Train Robbers
The Lawless Land
The Gambling Man
The Maverick
The Prairie Rat
Bullwhip
The Crooked Sheriff
The Montana Badmen
Lousy Reb
The Black Marshal
Blood Brothers
The Hanging of Cattle Kate
Bad Day at San Juan
Bushwhacked!
A Town Called Troublesome
Sidewinder
Horse Dreamer
The Horsehead Trail
Rogue Railroad
Canyon of Tears
Rattler
They Came to Riba
The Black Sheriff
Journey of Death
Two Shots for the Sheriff
Death at the Corral
The Lost Mine

# Stolen Horses

## JOHN DYSON

| CHESHIRE LIBRARIES | |
|---|---|
| | |
| Cypher | 22.08.04 |
| W | £10.75 |
| | 0405038/0012 |

A Black Horse Western

ROBERT HALE · LONDON

© John Dyson 2004
First published in Great Britain 2004

ISBN 0 7090 7521 9

Robert Hale Limited
Clerkenwell House
Clerkenwell Green
London EC1R 0HT

The right of John Dyson to be identified as
author of this work has been asserted by him
in accordance with the Copyright, Designs and
Patents Act 1988.

Typeset by
Derek Doyle & Associates, Liverpool.
Printed and bound in Great Britain by
Antony Rowe Limited, Wiltshire

# ONE

The cards were running as smooth as a mountain stream and for the first time in his young life Quince Simms felt he was on a roll and couldn't lose. The Travellers' Saloon on Squaw Creek was not a place he was familiar with; just a ramshackle joint, a rough-hewn bar selling raw whiskey and a poker game going on in a corner.

He was just passing through on his way along the south bank of the Red River valley, aiming to call in and see his folks. He had been away several months serving as horse wrangler on a cattle drive across the Red, north through Indian Territory to the railroad in Kansas. So, he had a few dollars in his pocket. He had stepped down to quench his thirst in the shady bar, leaving his horse, a rough-haired paint named Feathers, hitched outside. Maybe it was the worst decision of his life to buy a handful of fifty-cent chips and join that game

One game had just broken up and there were three players left, passing the bottle, grinning, counting their winnings, and they looked up at the youth who stood before them in a torn check shirt, worn blue jeans, sunbleached boots, jinglebob spurs and battered Stetson who said, 'Howdy, fellers. What's the game?'

They exchanged glances knowingly, assessing this fresh-faced youngster with his frank, grey eyes, his chin as yet hardly needing the touch of a razor. Maybe they figured him for an easy mark.

'Straight draw poker.' The one in the corner was a thickset, middle-aged man, his eyes bright and alert beneath the brim of his derby, a pugnacious nose protruding from a bushy black beard. 'No limit. You in, sonny?'

'Sure.' Quince took off his hat, pulled back a chair to sit opposite him, ran fingers through his fair hair, badly in need of a cut, and drawled, 'I'll play a while but I gotta be on my way 'fore dark. I got a fair piece to go.'

That had been high noon. Now the evening shadows were drawing in, the lanterns being lit. Quince was a tad worried about his horse, but he could not bring himself to leave the game. He spun a quarter to the bar boy to go feed Feathers a handful of split corn and loosen his cinch, and played on.

From the opening deal Quince had begun to win, raking in on pairs, straights and three of a kind. He could hardly believe his luck. The broad-of-beam guy in the corner, Zack, tried to put the hex on him, glowering malevolently, but equally steadily, *he* lost.

What Zack's profession was Quince had no idea, but his wan, waxy complexion and his pickled proboscis suggested he rarely left the purlieus of the saloon or the whiskey bottle alone.

The other two were scrawny country boys with sawtoothed drawls, down-at-heel no-goods by the look of them, and, from all accounts, brothers. They played with little finesse, taking their lead from Zack.

One of them, buck-toothed and sour-faced, named Sass, gave a whistle of awe as Quince won another hand. 'How's this boy do it?'

'That's what I'd like to know.' Zack eyed Quince suspiciously. 'Maybe he ain't the wrangler he claims to be. Maybe he's one of them gambler sharps we've heard about.'

'Boys, I'm as surprised as you. I ain't never been on a winning streak like this afore.' He doffed his palms wide and grinned at them. 'Look, I ain't got nuthin' up my sleeves.'

'Says you.' The other brother, Jesse, had a rash of acne across his face which he pulled into a malicious sneer. 'There's a fishy smell about you, pal, y'ask me.'

Quince got to his feet, hitching-up the buckle of his gunbelt. Like most men in those parts he carried a revolver slung on one hip, his being a Hopkins and Allen .38 he'd paid ten dollars for.

Zack growled in his husky voice, 'You ain't thinking of leaving this game?'

'Waal, like I said, I got a long stretch along the river to go tonight. But' – Quince consulted the barroom clock – 'I'll give you boys a coupla hours to try to win your cash back. Midnight I'm moseying on, come what may. I cain't say fairer than that.'

'So,' Sass squawked, 'where you goin' now?'

'Out back to take a leak. You wanna come and hold my hand?' Quince met his murky eyes and said, seriously, 'You might play better if you left that bottle alone.'

He ambled away, his spurs jingling, pushing through the throng, ignoring a sneering oath from Sass hurled at his back. Those three had been hitting the juice pretty hard and it was turning them nasty-tempered. Quince figured he had already raked in $200 in winnings. Outside, the stars were winking in the night sky. 'What I got to do,' he whispered to himself, 'is hang on to what I got then git outa this place fast.'

From the squeals of laughter issuing through the windows of the rooms above, it sounded as if the two-storey saloon also served as a cathouse. When he returned to the barroom Quince heard a shrill rebel yell from the top of the stairs and a voice shouted, 'Damn me! Look who it ain't. Quince Simms.'

A tall, handsome young dude, outfitted in a snazzy black shirt, pants, silver-studded boots and a black leather frock coat, was standing on the landing, smiling down at him. At first, Quince did not recognize him because he was wearing some kind of sun spectacles. 'Lance?' he asked, hesitantly. 'Is that you?'

'It sure as damn well is.' Lance Silverlight came leaping down the stairs two at a time and began mock-punching Quince to the body. 'How are you, old buddy?'

He hugged Quince to him and dragged him towards the bar. 'Come on, what's your poison? Whiskey?'

'Just a beer. I got to keep a clear head. I'm in a game. Them three over in the corner giving us the surly looks. And sure they should. I've just taken them for two hundred.'

'Two hundred!' Lance Silverlight gave a whoop and punched him again. 'In that case you're paying. Sling us a beer and a bottle of red-eye, 'keep.'

One reason why Quince hadn't recognized Lance was because he had shot up since they had been schoolkids together. 'How long is it, eight years since they threw us out?'

'Well, we were hardly ever there. Generally,' Lance said, 'we was off fishing or up to some mischief along the river.'

Another reason was that Silverlight's black hair now hung down shoulder-length beneath his wide-brimmed black hat and the silver-rimmed dark glasses imparted a somewhat sinister air to the planes of his deeply sun-tanned face. But his white-toothed, boyish smile made him instantly memorable.

'I seem to remember you were the one who was allus in trouble,' Quince grinned, as the glass of beer was slid along the bar top to his hand. He raised it to his mouth and took a sip. 'How's things, Lance?'

'Just the same. If there's trouble, I'm in it. Whoo! That Negress up there. She really knows how to work a man over. You should try her.'

'Yeah, you sure ain't changed. If I remember right you were after the girls even before you were eight.'

'Girls are like oxygen to me. I need 'em.' Lance gave his perfect smile. It was true. He had a way with the ladies and he knew it. 'Mind you, I don't usually have to pay for the pleasure. But you should invest two dollars in that gal Suzie. She's real hungry for it.'

As Lance began to itemize Suzie's abilities in lurid detail, Quince patted his shoulder and said, 'It's great seein' ya again, Lance, but I gotta be gettin' back to the game.'

'Hey, you know who they are?' Lance grabbed at his shirt. 'The Boltons. You better watch yourself, boy.'

'The Boltons?' The name had a faintly menacing sound to it. 'No, I cain't say I know them.'

'The meanest bunch of critters who prowl these parts.' Lance gave a crazy laugh. 'Apart from my own extended family, of course. If you think you're walking outa here with your cash, you're gonna have to watch your back.'

'You don't say.' Quince considered this and shrugged. 'Arr,' he scoffed, 'you're pulling my leg.'

'Don't say you ain't been warned. Hey, I tell you what. I'll come and sit in with you.' Lance threw back the skirt of his leather coat to reveal a Colt Lightning double action, the holster strung tight to his thigh. He lightly touched the staghorn butt. 'With me along they'll think twice afore robbin' you, boy.'

'I don't want no trouble, Lance.'

'Nobody wants trouble. It's bluff, ain't it? That's what poker's about.'

Before he could dissuade him, Lance had strode over to the table and taken a chair. 'Hiya, boys, deal me in.'

'No way.' Zack growled at him like a bear with a sore head. 'You think we're gonna let you two set us up? This is 'tween us and him.'

'Who is this dude?' Sass asked Quince. 'Another fancy card sharp? What you an' your pard tryin' to pull?'

'He ain't my pard. This is the first time I seen him since I was twelve,' Quince replied. 'You better stay outa this, Lance. OK, let's play.'

'You ain't got any objections if I sit here and watch,' Lance adjusted his sun spectacles and gave them his reckless grin. 'You fellas are a real ball of laughs.'

'Don't you go sendin' him any signals,' Jesse shouted, hotly. 'What you all dressed up like some whorehouse pimp for, anyhow?'

'Thass probably what he is,' Sass put in. 'I never did trust 'breeds.'

'I ain't no 'breed.' Lance spat his words out, equally hotly. 'No Injin, no Mex blood in me. I just tan easy. My ass is as white as snow. You want me to show it you?'

'Forget it, Lance. Come on, mister, deal.'

Even if he had tried to lose it seemed unlikely that he could tonight. Instead of decreasing, the pile of chips before him again increased. And as the hours passed, his opponents were getting more and more riled up. And the madder they got the worse they played.

Quince had only had a couple of steam beers and felt clear-headed, as cool as a cucumber. He could not restrain a leap of excitement in his blood for the cards had fallen his way again. 'Three queens,' he said, spreading his hand. 'I'm calling you.'

"'Dang and blast you.' Zack tossed down his hand with disgust. 'Where you gettin' 'em from? Last time it was four aces.'

'Looks like I win again.' Quince looked up at a small crowd of rubberneckers who were watching the game, a scruffy collection of cowpunchers and storekeepers. 'Beats me how I done it. It's just my lucky day, thassall.'

'Listen to him,' Sass sneered. 'This ain't right. He's dealin' from the bottom of the deck. And his pal's helping him.'

'Just be careful what you're saying, sunshine.' From behind the dark shades Lance was watching the bearded bozo. He was pretty sure he had a big old cap and ball revolver laid across his knees. 'I ain't got nuthin' to do with this game. And my friend's as honest as the day is long. He allus was. That's his downfall.'

Quince glanced at the clock. It was two a.m. There were only a few hard-drinkers left at the bar. The main customers had drifted away. He began to reach out to haul in his pile of chips. 'Well, I've given you a fair chance to win your money back. I got to be headin' on.'

'Yeah,' Lance put in. 'A good gambler knows when to quit. When he's winning.'

'You stay right where you are, you lousy snake,' Zack roared at Quince. 'You been playin' a crooked game. You ain't havin' none of them chips.'

'Mister, you're making a mistake,' Quince replied, freezing for seconds, swallowing his fear as he met the bearded man's angry, bloodshot eyes. 'I won this pot fair and square and I'm taking it out of here.'

'That's what you think.' Zack was fumbling beneath the table. 'You—'

Quince had risen to his feet, and it was fortunate for him that he had, for there was the flash and roar of an explosion as Zack cursed and fired from beneath the table. The company scattered as the slug ploughed between Quince's open thighs, smashing through the chair he had been sitting on seconds before.

Lance, too, was on his feet, the Colt Lightning in his fist as Zack tried to pull out the long-barrelled revolver from beneath the table for another shot. Silverlight aimed it, arm outstretched and shot the bearded man point blank through the heart. He watched him kick back in his chair, hitting the wall, jerking in convulsions, and carefully put two more slugs in him.

'That's the last time he'll call anybody a cheat,' Lance Silverlight said. 'Pick up your winnings, Quince. We're getting out of here.'

'Yeah, how about me?' The sour-faced Sass snatched up a sawn-off shotgun from the floor beside him. He brought it up, thumbing the hammer, but he had underestimated the speed of a double action. 'Shee-it,' was his last word as he, too, was taken out with a heart shot. He fell back, his shotgun blast peppering the ceiling.

By this time Quince had his .38 out. He swung the revolver to cover Jesse who was attempting to haul a stubby 'storekeeper' from his coat pocket. 'Don't do it, Jesse. Two dead's enough, ain't it?'

'You bastard,' Jesse was stammering, almost in tears, as black powdersmoke drifted around the barroom and men stood like statues, waiting and watching. 'You kilt my kin. I'll kill you.' Wildly, he dragged out his snubnose handgun and cocked it to fire, but screamed as Quince's bullet smashed through his shoulder.

Quince watched him collapse slowly back upon the burly, bloody Zack as the 'storekeeper' clattered to the floor. He heard Lance order, 'Finish him.'

Quince shook his head, stunned by the sudden turn of events. 'No, I don't want to kill him. I didn't start this.'

'No, but we gotta finish it.' Lance Silverlight turned his own gun on the fallen youth. 'He's—'

'No.' Quince knocked up the gun as Lance fired. 'Leave him.'

'What's the matter with you?' Lance sneered, but slowly slid the self-cocker back into its holster. 'Well, them other two sure cashed in their chips.'

'That's what you two had better do,' the barkeep said, as the folk in the saloon came back to life. 'Come on, I'll settle up with you. Then you better git outa here fast. Them three's got kin in this county. They'll come lookin' for you. North Texas won't be a safe place to be.'

'It was a fair fight,' a man said, patting Quince on the back. 'And a fair game. I was watching. You ain't got nuthin' to feel guilty about, son. Them two skunks ain't no loss to nobody and t'other looks like he's sinkin' fast.'

Quince did not reply. Dazed, he felt like he was in

another world to the onlookers. How had he got into this? It was the first gunfight he had ever been in. 'Jeez,' he groaned, as he examined the tear in his pants, the red bullet graze inside his right thigh just below his crotch. 'He nearly took off my balls!'

Everybody began to laugh at this. Maybe it was the relief after the tension. Lance was collecting his winnings in greenbacks from the 'keep. 'Come on,' he said, tucking the wad in Quince's shirt pocket. 'Let's ride, cowboy, 'fore the sheriff starts sticking his nose in here.'

Quince allowed himself to be tumbled out of the saloon, and climbed on Feathers, remembering to tighten the cinch. He touched his spurs to the paint and charged after Lance Silverlight as he went racing on his horse out of Squaw Creek.

## TWO

'There's been some shooting. I gotta clear out for a bit while it cools down.' Quince pressed a roll of one hundred greenbacks into the workworn hands of the thin woman in her faded dress. 'This is for you. You take care now, Ma.'

His mother waved the money away as if it might be contaminated. 'I don't want any tainted cash.'

'I won it honest, Ma. Only the fellas didn't like losing it. Go on, take it.'

She wiped a straggle of hair from her bony face and accepted reluctantly, gazing at him with stern, grey eyes. 'We ain't got much but what we got we worked for honestly.' She glanced along at Lance Silverlight who sat his black horse by the farm gate, a dark, foreboding figure waiting for him. 'Why you got mixed up with him? He allus was a bad influence.'

'He saved my life, Ma. If it weren't for him I'd be lying dead in that saloon.'

'You get away from him. His mother's a whore, his father's a weak fool for letting her be and his kin are worse. Don't let him talk you into anything.'

'So long, Pa.' Quince offered his hand to his father who, in his old work clothes stood by silently. 'I'll write sometime. I gotta go.'

'You heed your mother's words, boy,' Arthur Simms said. 'Don't do nuthin' to shame us. We done our best for you.'

'Sure, don't worry 'bout me.' Quince swung on to his piebald, spread his fingers to his two sisters and small brother who stood outside the cabin watching, and gave them a grin. 'See y'all.'

He turned the pony away and rode to the trail. There was a cold wind of early spring whipping the dust into their eyes. At the gate, he looked back at the forlorn group on their dirt-poor piece of land. They looked like ghosts silently accusing him.

'What a tender leave-taking,' Lance Silverlight scoffed. 'You ready?'

'Sure, let's ride.'

They drifted due south to Wichita Falls and on, crossing the west fork of the Trinity river, rolling on, day after day, like the tumbling tumbleweed, pausing to eat and rest awhile in small towns that dotted the vast expanse of Texas: Rising Star, Comanche, Mineral Wells and along the meandering Rio Brazos to Waco.

Quince had been brought up to be careful with his cash. He still had $130 left from his card win: four months pay to a cowboy. He generally avoided loose women and strong spirits and had vowed not to get in deep gambling again. The money should have lasted him awhile. But not the way Lance Silverlight spent it. 'Come on, pal,' he'd say, wheedling another ten dollars out of Quince to spend in the saloon. 'You know I'd do the same for you if I had it. We're pards, ain't we?'

Quince was keen to find himself another job on a ranch as wrangler or general hand. But somehow their reputation seemed to follow them. Nobody wanted a killer working on their spread. Lance Silverlight, trailing after him, in his black attire and sinister sunspecs, had all the looks of a professional gunslinger. 'No.' The rancher would shake his head. 'We ain't got nuthin' for you two.'

On they drifted, through Rosebud and Yegua Creek, camping out nights, swimming their horses across the Colorado, reaching San Marcos in the deep south of the Lone Star state. By this time most of their cash had gone.

It was in the bustling market town of San Antonio that Lance Silverlight teamed up with a Mexican youth known as One Eye Pedro. A cheerful character, he had lost his left eye in a knife brawl and sported a glass eye, green with yellow flecks, a real mismatch to his natural brown one. He had the disconcerting habit of being able to wink and squeeze out the glass one to let it roll along the bar counter leaving a gaping socket.

For Lance Silverlight, it was a useful trick, for it took attention off any sleight of hand he might be using to rearrange the cards in his favour. Quince knew they were cheating and warned them about it. 'Somebody's gonna spot you one of these days and it's gonna end bad.'

Quince had been seriously considering splitting

from them, but the crunch came when they were camped along San Miguel creek. He was crouched in his tattered sheepskin jacket tending to some flapjacks in their fire wondering where they'd got to when he heard them whooping and yelling. They came trotting through the dusk driving a small herd of cattle, about fifty head, which they rope-coralled along the creek.

'What the hell you up to?' Quince demanded. 'Where'd you get those?'

'We found 'em wanderin' on the prairie.' Silverlight sat his black, Beater, and flashed his reckless grin. 'Nobody seemed to wan' 'em.'

'Don't be stupid. What about those brands?'

'Don' worry, *amigo*,' Pedro called. 'I got a li'l brandin' iron. We can soon alter those.'

'Count me out of this.' Quince hauled up his saddle and slung it over Feathers. 'You know what they do to cattle or hoss-thieves around here? I ain't lookin' to kick air.'

'Aw, come on, Quince. Everybody does a bit of rustlin'. It's a Texan's second occupation. How else we gonna raise some cash?'

One Eye Pedro squatted down by the fire and poked the flapjacks out of the ashes. He made a high-pitched cackling sound, '….choo, chuck, chuck, chuck.'

Quince spun on him. 'Don't you call me chicken. Put up your damn fists, I'll show you who's chicken.'

For reply Pedro whipped out a revolver and aimed it at Quince. 'This is how I fight, white boy. Go on, clear out. We don' need you. But you spit bad about us to anybody you gonna answer to this. Savvy?'

'I ain't gonna blab to nobody,' Quince replied hotly. 'I just don't wanna know, thassall.' He reached to jerk tight his saddle's latigo strap, picked up his warbag and blanket roll to sling across the back of the saddle. 'No hard feelings, Lance, but I've had enough of this. You can consider our partnership severed. OK?'

'Sure, please yourself, Quince.' Lance Silverlight shrugged as he watched the wrangler mount up. 'Don't know what's got into you. We'll see you around.'

'I certainly hope not. I'd take them cattle back if I was you, Lance. Once you cross over the divide and turn rustler and outlaw there ain't no going back. You know that.'

'How else we gonna make a dollar?'

'You could try working for it. Thass how.' Quince climbed into the saddle and nudged Feathers away along the creek. 'Don't say I ain't warned you.'

He rode away into the falling night, Pedro's laughter and chicken cackling echoing in his ears. 'I've had enough of those damn fools,' he said.

Quince followed the creek until with the dawn he came to the confluence of the Atacosa and Neuces rivers and swam Feathers across to a township aptly named Three Rivers. A black blacksmith was clanging his hammer on iron and working the bellows of his furnace for the start of the day. 'How much to replace a loose shoe?' the youth asked.

'Three dollars,' was the reply, at which Quince

winced and asked, 'Can I owe it you?'

The big, muscular ex-slave turned to give him the once over. 'You broke, boy?'

'You could say. I'm seeking work as a wrangler. You know any place?'

'The biggest spread round these parts is the Circle Dot. Otherwise known as the Santa Esmeralda. Out on the trail due north. You can't miss it.' The black spoke without ceasing work. 'John Durham's a fair man.'

'Right.' Quince warmed himself from the night's cold at the fire. 'Know any way I might raise three dollars meanwhile?'

'Well, this damn barn could do with a lick of paint and the sign re-letterin'.' He grinned at Quince and raised the piebald's back hoof to hold between his knees, reaching for his pincers. 'There's cans of paint and brushes over in the corner. Sooner you git started sooner you're finished.'

'Right.' Quince eyed the coffee pot on the stove and the man said, 'Help yourself.'

'Thanks.'

'You on your own?'

'I am now. I had a falling out with my pals.'

'Why so?'

Quince sucked at the scalding brew. 'Oh,' he muttered. 'No reason.'

By late afternoon, he had finished the paint job and the smith gave him two dollars and his shoed horse for a good job done. A two-hour ride took him to the Santa Esmeralda and he liked the look of the whitewashed two-storey house, its corrals and outbuildings as soon as he saw it. Everything was neat and tidy, the fences in order, a remuda of feisty horses in the big corral, and the longhorn cattle he had passed *en route* well fed and tended. On top of which there was a tasty supper smell drifting from the cookhouse which made his mouth water and empty belly rumble.

Old Man Durham came out from the porch when he was called; a man of medium height, in range clothes, his face weatherbeaten and canny beneath a mop of white hair. He sported a thick white moustache and drawled, 'You lookin' for work, son?'

'Yessuh, as a wrangler. There ain't much about hosses I don't know.'

'We'll see about that. You see them calves in the corral over there? Go cut one out and castrate it.'

'Well, I'll try, but I gen'rally have someone to hold him down.'

'At least you know that much. Bull,' – when he hollered, a broader version of himself stumbled outside – 'we got a punk Texan here blowin' his own trumpet. Let's see if he's got any sap.'

'Right, Dad.' His eldest son glowered at Quince and ambled across to the corral. 'In you go, cowboy. I want that one with the black ear.'

Quince edged Feathers carefully towards the skittering bunch of calves, manoeuvring his horse forwards and backwards, turning him to cut off the calf, gently arranging his lariat in his right hand to toss deftly over its head. 'Gotcha,' he said, tying the rope to his saddle horn, swinging down with practised ease leaving Feathers to take the strain. He caught hold of the calf and hoisted it belly up on to his knee, thudding it down into the dust. 'OK,' Bull grunted, 'I got him.'

He sat on the beast's shoulders while Quince grabbed hold of its hind legs, holding it steady with an outstretched boot. He already had his scalpin' knife out and, quick as a flash, the job was done.

Bull anointed the wound with tecole grease and the calf scrambled away lamenting loudly to join the bunch. 'Hey, you ain't forgettin' these?' He grinned as he retrieved the testicles. 'Prairie oysters. Real tasty.'

'Looks to me like you know your stuff, young feller,' John Durham said. 'Pay's thirty a month all found.'

'How much land you got?' Quince asked.

'Far as the eye can see. We don't have no fences in this country. Bordered on two sides of the river, the rest by that range of hills. You come in the house I'll have you sign an agreement. OK?'

'This is new to me,' Quince said, as he entered the spacious 'drawing-room' of the ranch house and Durham produced a sheet of paper from the drawer of a desk. He stared blankly at it when it was handed to him. It was just a lot of squiggles to him. 'I ain't never had to—'

'Why don't you read it to him, Daddy?' a girl's voice broke in. 'Don't embarrass the poor boy. It's pretty obvious it's all Greek to him.'

Quince turned to meet the sparkling, merry eyes of the girl, a slim teenager younger than himself, and felt like he'd been hit by a heart shot. She was the prettiest little chickadee he ever did see, the blue-eyed fair-haired rancher's daughter, Marie Durham.

'Why don't you read it to him, Marie?' Durham pointed to the piece of paper. 'You must understand, Mr Simms, I've had trouble with various deadbeats so I've drawn up this list of rules you'll agree to abide by while you're in my employ.'

'Rule *Numero Uno*,' Marie sang out, in a faintly ironic manner. 'Card playing and gambling is strictly forbidden.'

'You needn't worry about that,' Quince muttered. 'I've solemnly promised my ma I'll give up poker.'

'Rule Two: employees are forbidden to indulge in intoxicating liquors, malt or spiritous, on the premises of the company.'

'You git one day off a month and can go raise hell in Three Rivers if you want,' the Old Man, as he was known, explained, 'but there'll be no drinking on my time.'

'Rule Three: No employee is allowed to run any horses or cattle on the company's land.'

'What about Feathers?' Quince was in a daze. All he could do was stare at Marie Durham as if he'd been struck by lightning. 'He's my hoss.'

''That's allowed,' Durham said. 'It's just that I've had certain young scallywags building up little herds of their own from my stock. Any such activity means instant dismissal.'

'Rule Four: loafers, sweaters, deadbeats, tramps, gamblers, or any person suspected of unlawful activities are not to be entertained on company land by any employee.'

'That means, you got any bad hat pals, we don't want 'em near here," Durham scowled.

'Rule Five: company employees must not use swear words within earshot of the ranch's womenfolk and must try to refrain from such language at other times.'

The rancher looked even more severe. 'That's just to warn you that you treat my wife and daughter here with the utmost respect at all times. You can address this young lady as Miss Marie.'

'Oh, Dad, you don't need to say this. Quince, I'm sure, is a real nice and polite young man.'

'Yeah – well – he'd better be. OK, skip the other rules. Sign at the bottom, Quince. Or put your mark.'

'I can sign my name.' Quince struggled with the pencil. 'That's just about all, though. Guess I spent too much time playin' hookey when I was a kid.'

'Right, that's it.' John Durham took the paper, put it back in a drawer. 'The bunkhouse is t'other side of the yard. Supper's served in the cookhouse any time soon.'

'Nice to meet you, Quince.' The girl offered cool, slim fingers and smiled, dazzlingly. 'I hope you'll like it here.'

'It ain't liking, it's workin' he's here for. From sunrise to sunset and you'll be expected to ride herd at nights. We don't entertain no slackers.'

'There's one thing I ought to tell you,' Quince blurted out. 'You're being straight with me so I want to be straight with you.'

'Spit it out, young fella. You been in trouble of some sort?'

'Yeah.' He almost gasped out the word, fearing the worst. 'It was a place called Squaw Creek. I got in a card game. Two men got killed by my pal and I put a bullet in the shoulder of another. I promise you it was self-defence.'

'So, you're an associate of a killer and you're on the lam?'

'Yes – uh – I guess it looks like that.'

The Old Man went across to the fireplace and pondered this. 'You've given me a problem. Normally, I'd say, sorry, son, you're out. But will you give me your word you've broken with this man and all that?'

'Yessuh, I definitely have. I don't wanna be involved in anything like that, no suh, no more, never again.'

'OK, I'm gonna give you a chance to prove yourself, Quince. But if I get the slightest suspicion you're consorting with criminals or stepping out of a line—'

'You've no need to worry, Mr Durham. All I want is a chance to prove myself.'

'Well, times are hard, boy. But I'll do good by you if you do good by me.'

# THREE

Lance Silverlight and One Eye Pedro had doctored the brands of the forty-odd head of cattle they had commandeered and drove them south until they reached the Neuces River. It was hard, dusty work and Lance was feeling a little edgy, eager to get rid of them. It was true what Quince had told them: many a rustler had met a premature end swinging from a branch with a noose around his neck.

It was the start of the 1880s and things had changed since the end of the Civil War when men like John Durham could mark out their territory, free land as far as the eye could see, and thousands and thousands of scrubby longhorns running wild. Nowadays most of the land in this corner of Texas was owned by the big spreads and they guarded their stock vigilantly.

Their small bunch had settled down nicely by the water and would not need much watching. 'What we gonna do with 'em now?' Lance asked, as he stretched out against his saddle by their camp-fire.

'Eet ees only a hundred miles or so to the Mexican

border. We can easy sell them in Laredo.'

'Aw, hell. Go all that way, cross the Rio Grande? What for, a few pesos? Surely we can find some sonuvagun around here looking to increase his stock, no questions asked?'

'It vair risky sell north of border 'til them brands have grown in,' Pedro mused.

'Yeah, and it's risky hanging on to 'em much longer around here.' Lance gobbled down a mess of beans Pedro had cooked up and tossed the tin plate away. 'But how else is a man gonna raise himself any cash these days? Ol' Quince ain't never goin' to git rich by bein' honest. Fancy that yellow-bellied, goody-goody runnin' out on us like that? I had high hopes for that boy.'

'He don' understand.' Pedro grinned at him as he rolled a cigarette and lit up. 'We ain't really stealin', we are just taking from them who have got too much.'

'Sure, how else can a young feller make a start for himself?'

In the morning, Lance stayed to guard the stock while Pedro scouted along the Neuces towards Oakville. And, indeed, he did find a small-time nester, who returned with him to examine the beasts with a jaundiced eye.

The ragged man puffed at his brier pipe and asked, 'How d'ye come by 'em?'

'We bought 'em, mister,' Lance said, breezily. 'But we decided we don't wanna go into the cattle business after all. They're yours, three dollars a head full-grown, a dollar the calves.'

'You got a bill of sale?'

'Unfortunately,' Lance smiled, 'I lost it.'

'Waal,' the man drawled, 'you can give *me* one. Twenty bucks the whole shebang. Take it or leave it. That's all I got.'

Twenty dollars was twenty dollars and Silverlight put a phoney signature to a receipt the scrawny fellow scrawled out in pencil to cover himself.

'Hey, *hombre*,' Lance yelled, jumping on to Beater, 'let's go celebrate. I told you there's allus some sonuvagun waiting around the corner to part with his cash.'

They set off to look for the nearest saloon which happened to be an adobe shack on a bend of the river, a one-horse watering hole called Crannock's Crossing.

Some time later they were sitting outside, sprawled on a bench, enjoying the warmth imparted by homebrewed potato lightning plus the effulgent rays of the setting sun, when they noticed a plume of dust on the horizon. Silverlight was doubly pleased because by maladroit manipulation of his pack of marked cards he had managed to cheat a couple of dimwitted carrot-pickers out of another twenty dollars.

'*Amigo*, I no weesh to jolt you from your pleasant mood, but I got the feelin' them riders headin' hell for leather across the plain towards us ain't friendly inclined.'

'What you talkin' about, One Eye?'

'I mean' – the Mexican had already tightened the cinch on his grey and swung into the saddle – 'they look like a lynch party.'

'Hell!' Lance Silverlight cried out, and tumbled off the bench as a bullet smashed into the wall, where, a few seconds before, his head had been as he enjoyed the peaceful idyll of the setting sun. 'I believe you.'

He scrambled up, grabbed hold of Beater and sent him racing away, hanging on to the saddle horn to swing himself on to his back to follow Pedro who was racing away along the river-bank.

Fortunately, dusk was fast descending which made it easier to give the irate posse of cattlemen the slip. At first, after splashing across the river ford, Lance wondered why Pedro was turning back the way they had come but on the far bank to the pursuers. It was risky, as carbine lead flew about their heads, but they galloped on grimly, returning the leaden compliments with their own guns.

Pedro, of course, was as crafty as a fox. The cowmen had to ride up to the crossing, which gave the young rustlers a good start. Soon they had put half a mile between them and raced on down the far bank of the winding river. It was suddenly dark as the moon had yet to rise. When they had galloped around the sweeping bend of the river, Pedro pulled hard in beneath a clump of cottonwood trees. Lance joined him and they watched and waited.

'Neat!' Silverlight cried, as, with a drumming of hooves, the half-dozen men went charging by. 'Where to now?'

'Back the way we come.' Pedro grinned at him from beneath the shadow of his big sombrero. 'Weeth any luck they go chasin' half-way to Mexico.'

They took to the hills to give Crannock's Crossing a wide berth, climbing up steep, rocky mountainside behind the Neuces Canyon, and ploughed down through the shale on the other side, the soaring moon lighting their way at last. They rode so wildly it was only by luck one of their mounts did not stumble and break a leg. It was a good short cut, however, saving many miles around the loop of the river. Soon they had rejoined the Neuces River and at dawn rode into the small settlement of Oakville.

On the outskirts was a rickety cottage of shiplap boards run as a lodging house by a widow lady of Pedro's acquaintance. They put the horses in her stable, wiped them down, and went to hammer on her front door.

'What's all the fuss and palaver?' a reedy voice quavered, as the door was unbolted and creaked back to reveal the bony face beneath a silver-haired bun of an ancient lady, a cat perched on the hump of her back, 'Aw, it's you, you varmint, is it?'

'*Si*, Señora Allen, we need to rest up today.'

'Travellin' by night now, are ye? What you been up to? No, don't tell me.'

She blinked rheumy eyes at them, but shuffled off to her kitchen to boil up coffee, and fry slices of ham for breakfast, liberally laced with cat's hairs. The only other lodger was a drunken former sea captain, Mr Mundeliers, who never went out until dark. They would be safe enough. Lance and One Eye slept with the peace of angels throughout the day in her double bed. They even took off their boots.

'They ain't gonna be making us kick clouds yet,'

Lance bragged, when he roused himself about four and shaved with his cut-throat razor. 'Life might well be short but I'm gonna eat, drink and make merry. Live for the present, that's my motto. I got a lot of livin' and lovin' to do.'

The widow served more cat's hairs for supper on their steaks. They paid her two dollars and went out back to saddle their broncs.

'Let's take a look at Three Rivers,' Silverlight said. 'Who knows what we might find.'

Rancher John Durham had carried a musket in the Big War from the age of fourteen for the Union side all the way from Bull Run to the surrender. He had been lucky to survive unscathed and had earned his sergeant's chevrons. But he had returned to his Kentucky home to find his farmhouse had been laid waste by Nathan Forrest's raiders. So he, his wife and two young boys, Bull and Jesse, had packed what they could salvage on to a wagon and headed West. Or, more accurately, out into the great south-west of Texas where Comanches still roamed, but were being punished and pushed back by the Rangers. There were thousands of wild longhorns in the scrub. Most men hunted them for their hides, but Durham, and other pioneers, had the foresight to see there was a market in the north-east hungry for beef. But how would they get the beasts to that market?

Word reached them that the railroad had reached Abilene on the plains of Kansas and a man called McCoy was building pens and loading ramps and would pay cash for all the beeves he could buy. Thus had begun the great cattle drives, sweeping up through Texas, crossing wide rivers, like the Red, blazing a trail through Indian Territory, cattle dying of thirst or going blind in the drought, stampedes, rustlers, hostile Indians and settlers to deal with as they crossed their land. If a cowboy completed one of these drives he was counted a real man. John Durham had made a dozen in his time, joined by his sons as they grew up, and he had grown rich in the cattle boom.

To some it seemed odd that a Union man had settled in Confederate heartland but Durham got on well with his neighbours, merely referring to the war as 'our recent unpleasantness'. He was respected for his toughness, honesty, hard work and canny judgement.

He had been keeping an eye on Quince and in the few days he had been working on the Circle Dot he could see that he was an expert wrangler for sure. Just the man to put in charge of his remuda of sixty horses gathered ready for this summer's great trek northwards to sell more longhorns. Durham liked each of his cowboys to have seven or eight horses to use in rotation on the day-long drives and night-herding. They could not survive the ordeal with less.

At breakfast he was being badgered by his daughter, Marie, to be allowed to drive into Three Rivers to pick up a new dress she had had fitted and to collect some supplies. 'Me and the boys are busy out on the range,' Durham replied, grumpily. 'You ain't drivin' in on your own. I'll tell the new kid, Quince, to drive you. You can pick me up some baccy and bullets while you're there.'

So Quince was more than pleasantly surprised when he was told to harness the light rig. He had had Marie constantly on his mind for days and his heart began thumping at the prospect of being close to her, and alone together, most of the day. Up to now he had never been much of a ladies' man, but as soon as he had looked into Marie's sparkling eyes he had fallen hook, line and sinker. Now was his opportunity, perhaps, to show her how he felt.

'Hi!' she called, as he drew the high-stepping filly up outside the steps to the ranch-house door. 'What a lovely day.' She was just a slim teenager, younger than he, but she had all the cocksure authority that her position as the boss's daughter gave her. 'So, I've got a new driver. This should be fun.'

'Well, Miss Marie, it'll certainly be that for me and an unexpected pleasure.' Quince tried to be casual and gallant at the same time, without revealing too obviously that he was in thrall to her charms. 'Let's go shall we?'

Marie was wearing a summer dress of plain blue, tight at the waist and bodice, which revealed her suntanned, shapely calves in white ankle socks and sandals. There was something about her eyes, the blue irises intensified by dark aureoles, that pierced him to the core, and her intelligent, angular face that made his head whirl. And something wild and feline about her slim body that stirred his blood.

Her ash-blonde hair was drawn back in a headband, but it hung in a long mane silkily catching the morning light. He wanted to just sit and stare at her as she climbed up beside him on the box. But he gulped back his emotions, flicked the whip over the filly's ears and cried, 'Yip!'

It was indeed a fine morning to be sprinting along on the high-wheeled surrey across the prairie, weaving through the longhorns who were being brought in from the range for the big trail north.

'Will you be going with them, Quince?' Marie asked.

'Yeah, I guess so. Looks like I'll be away three months or more.'

'Aw, gee. I'll miss you, Quince.'

His heart leapt at the girl's unexpected words. 'Waal, I barely know you, Miss Marie, but I'll miss not seeing you somethang awful, too.'

'Really?' She gave him a lingering smile and pressed closer. 'There's no need for all that "miss" business when the Old Man ain't around.' She tucked her fingers under his arm to steady herself as they wheeled along. 'Just call me Marie. You know, when I first met you, Quince, I had the feeling you were going to be a true friend.'

'I sure hope so, Miss ... er ... I mean, Marie.'

'You know you said you couldn't read. I been thinkin', if you like, if you ever get any spare time, I could give you lessons, help you with your letters. You seem a bright boy, Quince. It seems a shame not to be able to read.'

'That's my own fault. My misspent childhood.' He grinned and glanced at her. 'But that would be really great, if you could. Would it be OK with Mister Durham?'

'Aw, you don't want to worry about him. He's an old softie at heart. I can twist him around my finger.' She gave a tinkling laugh. 'All those rules and regulations of his. You don't need to take them too seriously.'

'Don't I?' He was confused by her words. 'But I signed a contract and I gotta abide by it.'

'Have you?' She gave him a teasing smile. 'Well, you do what you think's right.'

He became a tad tongue-tied at that. All he wanted to do was haul the rig in under a cottonwood tree, take her in his arms and kiss her lips. But hadn't he given his word that he would show utmost respect to the rancher's daughter? Could he dare do such a thing and chance the consequences? Too late! By the time he had ceased debating this they had reached the main trail alongside the river and the township was fast coming into sight. He savoured the touch of her fingers on his arm and thought, maybe on the way back I'll tell her how I feel, I *will* do....

'Waal, lookee who's here. If it ain't ole Quince.' His heart sank as he heard the voice. He was manoeuvring the rig up alongside the hitching rail on one side of the dusty main drag of Three Rivers. 'And he's got hisself a purty gal.'

He looked up and saw Lance Silverlight standing on the raised sidewalk in his black leather frock coat and dark sun-spectacles with their silver-flashing frames. One Eye Pedro was sitting on a barrel behind him chewing on a bag of cashews. '*Si, bueno!*' Pedro pursed his lips, kissed his raised fingers. 'Where he find this beautiful *señorita?*' He began making a whistling and clucking sound, gripping his raised fist.

'This is my boss's daughter, Marie Durham. I would ask you to treat her with due respect.' Quince blushed, angrily, jumping down with the intention of walking round to help Marie descend. But, by the time he'd reached the filly's head, he saw that Lance had stretched out an arm to take Marie's hand and help her leap lightly to the sidewalk where, with gross familiarity, he swung her around to hold in one arm. 'Steady there,' Silverlight was saying. 'I wouldn't want a sweetie like you to slip.'

To Quince's chagrin, although she had tossed her hair, haughtily, Marie seemed to be making no serious objection to his former friend giving her a squeeze. In fact, her cheek had dimpled, mischievously, as she asked, 'Do you two know each other?'

'Me an' young Quince go way back. We sat on hay bales in the same soddy school. I guess you could say it was me led him astray.'

'Well, you ain't leadin' me astray no more.' Quince had joined them and was trying to capture Marie's attention. 'I got me a darn good job on Marie's father's ranch and I'm stickin' to it.'

'Maybe,' Marie suggested, 'if you boys are out of work Daddy would hire you, too.'

'I don't think Lance would care to sign up under the Old Man's rules,' Quince said, hoping to quash such an idea. 'No drinking, no cussin', no gambling, no running your own stock.'

'What is it?' Lance asked. 'Some kinda hermitage?'

'No gambling,' Pedro echoed. 'What the hell you do at nights?'

'I sure know what I'd like to do.' Lance gave his lecherous smile, doffed his hat, flicked back his long hair with a jerk of his head, and pulled the girl closer to him as if he was about to ravish her there and then.

'Excuse me, sir,' Marie said, and twirled away. 'I have shopping to do.'

'Lance ain't interested in hard work,' Quince muttered, somewhat bitterly.

'What for, a cowpoke's pittance?' Lance continued to regard her steadfastly through his long lashes. 'Young lady, I should point out I am a gentleman of independent means. I don't work for that kind of money.'

'Dear me, I hope I haven't offended you.' Marie shrugged and turned to Quince. She fumbled in her handbag and produced a list. 'Dad wants these things, bullets and some shag. Would you be a dear, while I go see about my fitting? And perhaps water the filly and stand her in the shade, then fetch a couple of sacks of flour for Mother.'

'Yes, Quince,' Lance agreed, loftily. 'You get about your duties, boy. I'll be glad to help Marie here with her parcels.'

Quince's jaw dropped as he watched Marie laugh and twirl away accompanied by the tall, long-haired Texan, saw him turn his dark, perfect profile to hers and make with his flashing, conceited smile, which, he knew, turned girls' knees to jelly. Yes, Quince had been hit by Cupid's arrow, OK. He felt like he was falling backwards down into some dark hole where he would be imprisoned, tongue-tied for ever. 'Well, I'll be damned—'

'Tut! Tut!' One Eye Pedro waggled a finger at him. 'You know you agreed to be a good boy. No swearing.'

By the time Quince caught up with them they were coming out of the ladies' haberdasher's, Marie radiant in her new purple and white candy-stripe dress, ankle length, and a little flower-bedecked hat perched on her head. 'Look what Lance has bought me,' she exclaimed. 'A new hat.'

'Bully for him,' Quince muttered.

By the time they had wandered along to the town restaurant for coffees, apple pie and cream, Lance Silverlight had become the main attraction and it was obvious to Quince that he was merely the gooseberry fool.

'Hadn't we better be gittin' back?' he asked, irritably, as they whispered and canoodled together. 'We got a long drive.'

It was, indeed, a long, silent drive back to the ranch, Quince wanting to blurt out his anger and feelings, but unable to. When they pulled into the ranch buildings, Marie announced another jaw-dropper. 'I've invited Lance to tea with Mother,' she cooed. 'I'd love her to meet him.'

'That's not a good idea.'

'What?'

'He's not for you. He's wild. I know him. He's a rollin' stone. There's no way you're goin' to tame him, Marie.'

'Why, Quince!' She stared at him, wide-eyed. 'I do believe you're jealous.'

'Maybe I am.' He reached out to grip her hands. 'But I love you, Marie. I can't help it. I've got to tell you. I'm in love with you. Lance can only bring you heartache and trouble. Believe me.'

'So, what can *you* offer me, Quince? I'm touched by your words. But, really!' Marie wrinkled her nose disdainfully, before twisting the knife in him harder. 'Lance comes from a rich ranching family. He told me so. He and I, we're made for each other.'

The girl jumped down and headed for the ranch house, turning on the steps to say, 'I'm sorry, I really am. But that's the way it has to be.'

When she had gone Quince gave a profound sigh. 'Jesus,' he groaned. It was his first acquaintance with overmastering passion and it was not a happy one.

# FOUR

A sickle of moon hazed by a scud of cloud cast enough light to enable the rider on his black bronc to see his way across the range towards the white wooden ranch house; enough light to ensure his fiery horse didn't put a hoof down a gopher hole and throw them both; enough to detect the shapes of the thousand head of longhorns, some down on all fours sleeping, others upright discontentedly lowing. Lance Silverlight moved Beater gently through without ruffling them. The herd was stretched a mile or so across the plain and he could see the shadowy shapes of a few night-herders as they rode their ceaseless circle.

'Whoa there, boy,' he murmured, as he noticed the pinprick red glow of a cigarette giving away the position of one of the drovers a hundred yards off. Lance loosened the Lightning in the leather holster on his thigh. If the worst came to the worst one blast would put the herd into a stampede and cover his getaway. But he didn't need to. The cowboy, softly crooning some old Texan ballad, ambled on his way.

Perhaps he hadn't seen him.

Silverlight favoured black clothing partly because he liked the style, but mainly because it was a good disguise when he went adventuring at nights. Lance nudged the mustang forward towards the lights of the house. It was midnight.

He halted his horse beneath a big oak beside the corral, slipping a black-gloved hand over his nostrils to prevent him snickering to the stock there. He peered at the ranch house wondering if the coast was clear. There were lanterns glowing in the upstairs windows, one of which was suddenly doused. A faint light, too, from the bunkhouse across the way where the cowboys not on duty would be snoring like pigs. Lance felt a frisson of excitement at being a lone intruder into this other world. From an early age he had loved to be out on the prowl.

'Hey,' he muttered to himself, 'that's some horse-flesh.' There were at least sixty mustangs skittering around the corral alerted by his approach. Horseflesh in fine fettle, worth a dollar or two. 'Good job I'm on a neighbourly call or I might be having a few of you.'

But Silverlight was not there to steal, unless one counts a heart. It was other flesh he was seeking, urged on by the need to have a young female in his arms. Sure enough, there she was, waiting.

'Lance,' the young girl's voice queried softly out of the darkness. 'Is that you?'

Marie Durham could see only the silhouette of the rider, the Stetson, the black leather frock coat, the butt of the Spencer carbine stuck up from the saddle boot. He rode up closer and she saw the gleam of his white teeth in the pale moonlight.

'Why, who the hell you think it is? Another of your gentlemen callers?'

'Don't be silly.' She ran to him as he leaped from his horse and they snaked arms around each other, lips meeting, hungrily. 'Oh, God,' she sighed, as the long kiss ended. 'I thought you'd never come. You know there's never been no one but you.'

Waal, Lance thought, I can't say the same, but maybe this could be the real thing? Maybe it could be for keeps? She was a pretty li'l peach just waiting to be plucked. Her daddy was rich. She could cook and sew and read and do most anything. Maybe it was time he settled down, and she would make a nice little wife.

'Do you really love me?" she murmured, kissing him again. 'Tell me. Was it really like you said when you first saw me in town, like a thunderbolt had struck? It *was* for me.'

'Well, a man ain't likely to make up a story like that, is he? Enough to risk my hide riding in here under cover of darkness like some damn rustler.'

Marie had stayed awake after the household went to bed, then had climbed out her window down the bough of a cottonwood, like she had when she was a kid. She was in a loose Spanish peasant blouse and skirt. 'I'm scared my daddy'll see us,' she whispered. 'He's told me if he ever catches me with some wild, wanderin' cowboy, he'll shoot him down like a skunk.'

For reply, Lance scooped her up under her arms

and legs and carried her into the barn. 'We'll be safer in here,' he said, laying her down on a bed of hay and falling upon her to kiss her some more.

Marie gasped for breath and told him, 'He says the only man who will ever have me is one from a solid worthwhile family with at least twenty thousand dollars in the bank.'

That's what *he* thinks, Silverlight thought. 'Very wise of him,' he murmured, as his fingers explored her blouse for the tips of her breasts. 'We got nuthin' to worry about, have we, sweetheart? That describes my family to a T.'

Marie was a bit breathless and distressed by the urgency of his loving. She had never intended to go so far, but his hands seemed to be getting everywhere. She tried to push him away, slow him down. 'Honey, are you serious about wanting to marry me? Only Quince said you'll never settle down.'

'Aw, don't you worry about him.' Lance nibbled at her ear lobe. 'He'd say anything to stop me having you. How much did you say your dowry was?'

'Five thousand dollars. Would your family think that's enough? I know they're plenty wealthy.'

'Yeah, I guess it'll do for a start. Enough to set us up on a little place of our own until my own inheritance comes through.' He pressed his attack, running his fingers up her thighs, trying to ease down her cotton pantalettes. 'Come on, baby, what're you worried about? We'll be married in a week or two.'

'No, Lance,' she protested. 'I want to keep myself for you for our wedding night. Please, don't!'

'Aw, come on, baby, can't you tell what you're doin' to me? What difference will a coupla weeks make?' If she'd been any other wench Silverlight would have given her a sharp slap or two to make her see sense. But there was a lot at stake. He guessed he would have to sweet-talk her if he wanted her to succumb. It might take longer but he had all night.

At two in the morning Quince Simms grabbed his hat, notched tight his gunbelt and stepped out of the bunkhouse. It was hot and fusty in there. He had been tossing and turning unable to sleep, his mind obsessed with images of Marie Durham. It was good to get out in the cool of the night, the moon riding high. He had to go relieve one of the night watch. He walked over to the corral to saddle a horse and, as he passed the barn, he came face to face with Lance Silverlight.

'What the hell you doin' here?' he asked.

Lance gave a smirk, pulling on his coat, tipping his black hat over his nose. 'You'd be surprised.'

'You better answer my question. You after our horses?'

'It ain't hosses interest me, Quince. Keep your voice down. I jest been payin' a social call.'

'Marie?' Quince gulped back his surprise when the slim girl stepped out from behind him. Her pale hair was ruffled, her blue eyes distraught, and she was brushing straw from her blouse. 'Are you all right?'

'Quince,' she whispered, huskily, 'don't make a fuss. Don't say anything to anybody about this, I beg you. I'm fine, Lance is just going.'

'He won't say nuthin' or he'll have me to deal with.' Lance took her hand and swaggered with her to the big cottonwood, picking her up and helping her into the branches. Quince had followed dumbly and noticed a dark patch like blood on the back of her skirt. As she climbed towards her window, Lance called, softly, 'So long, sweetheart.'

When she was safely inside, he turned to Quince and grinned as he slapped his shoulder. 'And so long to you, old buddy. Remember you gotta be a gentleman. Not a word.'

'Damn you.' Quince pushed his arm away. 'What you done to her, you bastard? You get outa here fast. And I don't want to see you back here again. You ain't for her. Leave her alone, for Christ's sake, Lance.'

'Oh, I'll be back. I've been invited to tea with her mama tomorrow. In fact, I might well be in the position to give you orders pretty soon. So you better watch yourself, cowboy.'

Dismayed, Quince watched him go, saw him swing on to the black and hightail it away, heard his mocking laughter as he disappeared into the darkness. 'Damn him,' he cursed. 'Damn him to hell.'

At three in the afternoon, Lance Silverlight rode up to the Santa Esmeralda ranch house as brazen as could be. It was deathly quiet and he guessed Old Man Durham, his sons, Quince and the boys would be out on the range gettin' the critters rounded up and branded.

Marie emerged from the porch looking as pretty

as a picture in her new candy-stripe dress, as bright-eyed and fresh as a daisy, as they say. 'Hi, honey,' he drawled, stepping down to squeeze her hand. 'Are you OK?'

'Yes, fine. I feel like a different person.' She smiled up at him. 'I was worried you wouldn't come.'

'Aw, you can allus rely on me to turn up like a bad penny.' He grinned at her, flicking his long hair out of his eyes. 'So, where's your ma?'

'Come on in.' She took him into the drawing-room. 'Mama, this is Lance I was telling you about. He helped me with my parcels in the town.'

The square-jawed Olga Durham nodded, her blue eyes glinting. 'Nice to meet you, Mr Silverlight.'

Of Swedish stock, she had married John Durham when he first arrived in Texas after the war. Her daughter had inherited her blue eyes and hair the colour of white gold. But the two sons had more of their father's dark and dogged taciturnity.

She bade him sit down and poured tea from her best teapot into china cups. She was favourably impressed by his good looks and polite manners. He didn't pour his tea into the saucer and blow on it like some cowpokes might do. After a bit of small talk, she ventured, 'I hear you're down this way on business.'

'Yeah.' Silverlight gave her his frank smile. 'I've been lookin' to gather some horses.' Generally, he thought, the misappropriation of them without payment. 'There's been a shortage this year due to the epizootic disease.'

'I take it you're one of the Silverlights, the big

ranching family up in north Texas.'

'Yes, that's true. The eldest son.'

Well, it *was* true. His family *was* big. His mother never seemed to cease popping 'em out, generally by different men she'd picked up in the saloons. And they had a dusty bit of ground along by the Red, a couple of cows and a few scrawny pigs. So they *were* ranchers, in a way.

'I'll come into everything. My daddy's ailing, I fear. Yes, we've got quite a spread though I don't like to brag about it.'

'Merit cuts little figure in love affairs,' Mrs Durham remarked, as she passed a tray of fancy cakes Marie had baked and iced, herself. 'A girl will often snub a dozen good men to fawn over a penniless fool. I'm so glad Marie has had the good judgement to choose a man of solid worth. Because, quite frankly, Mr Silverlight, it seems she has become enamoured of you.'

'And I of her, Mrs Durham,' Lance replied quickly. 'It was one of those things. A bolt from the blue. In fact, that's why I'm here. I'd like to hitch my wagon to hers.'

'You mean, marry her? It's awfully sudden. But I guess it *is* time she was wed.' And, she thought, best not to let a fish like this slip through their fingers. 'You seem a worthy suitor.'

'He's the man I love, Mama,' Marie cried. 'That's all there is to it. We want to marry as soon as possible.'

'It's not just an infatuation?'

'Hey, no, Mrs Durham. We're talking the real thang here.'

'Call me Olga, Lance.' He was a handsome young devil, that was for sure. She might not have been averse to him, herself, if she weren't happily married. 'I'll have to speak to her father about this tonight.'

'Good.' Lance rose to shake her hand. 'I'd like to make the wedding in a week or so. Don't want to rush Marie into it, but, like you, we're gonna be real busy pretty soon sending the cattle north.'

As Lance went out to unhitch Beater, squeezing Marie's waist and giving her a wink before he jumped aboard, her brothers, Bull and Jack rode in.

'This is my fiancé, Lance Silverlight,' Marie said, proudly. 'He's come to ask for my hand in marriage.'

'Oh, yeah?' Bull grunted, giving him the once-over. 'What's he after? Our money?'

'It's not something that bothers me, gentlemen,' Lance said with a smile, turning his horse away. 'I look forward to meeting your father pretty soon.' He raised a hand as he rode away. '*Adios*, y'all.'

Quince had another sleepless night wrestling with his conscience. Wasn't it his duty to warn the Durhams about Lance Silverlight? But Marie had begged him to remain silent. Maybe Lance could make her happy? What right had he to intervene? And, it went against the grain to betray an ole *compadre*....

But, by morning John Durham had taken matters into his own hands. He dispatched his youngest son, Jack, on the four-horse stage that headed north every day calling at San Antonio, Waco and Fort Worth. The Silverlights ranched near there at a place called Grand Prairie. By the end of the week Jack was back.

'Lance Silverlight,' he drawled, 'ain't the man he says he is.'

Silverlight was sprawled in the Hornet Saloon in Three Rivers splitting a bottle of tequila with One Eye Pedro Ocampo, explaining the situation some days later. 'I got her wound round my finger,' he said. 'My friend, I am marryin' rich. Her mammy's agreed. All she has to do is win over the Old Man.'

'You no meet with heem yet. He a tough ole buzzard.'

'No.' Lance was a bit perplexed why he'd had no approach from Durham. 'I bumped into the two brothers. They ain't 'zactly friendly so-an-so's. I got the distinct impression they thought I was after her dowry.'

'So, aren't you?'

'Well, yeah, that helps. But it's Marie. I really like that gal. I could almost say – yeah – it's love.'

'You surprise me, *amigo*. I theenk you ride anytheeng that bucks.'

'In the old days, maybe, but a man can't spend his whole life wanderin' and wenchin', livin' on his wits, harried from pillar to post. It's time I settled down. A man needs money behind him, and this is one way to git it, easy and legal. Of course, once I'm married, and rich, I won't be 'zactly hogtied. There'll allus be plenty of li'l serving gals.'

Lance rocked back in his chair, his long legs stuck out in their Lone Star emblazoned boots. He drew his eight-inch-barrelled Lightning, spinning the cylinder to check its load. 'I sure fooled them two ole brothers.' He gave Pedro his mocking, Southern-boy smile. 'I told 'em my family was plenty rich an' I weren't int'rested in Marie's cash.'

Pedro tipped more tequila into their tumblers and took a pinch of salt. 'They swallow that?'

'Sure did.' Silverlight's bragging smile suddenly faded. 'Jeez! Talk of the devil. Here they come now.'

Bull and Jack Durham looked like a couple of prowling wolves, their jaws set, grim and forbidding, as they strode into the saloon. They were roughly attired, dusty and dishevelled, as if they'd just ridden in off the range. And both were toting weapons, Bull a carbine, Jack a twelve gauge. Behind them stepped Quince, his revolver holstered, but looking equally serious.

'Thought we'd find you here, you no-good, whiskey-swillin' lecher,' Bull Durham shouted. 'We come to give you an ultimatum. Git outa town.'

'Yeah,' his brother Jack growled, 'an' stay out for good. We see your face round here we'll shoot you down like a dog.'

'Fellows.' Lance raised his hands, trying to pacify them. 'What's gotten into you? What's wrong?'

'You're wrong. That's what's wrong,' Bull said. 'You tryin' to kid us you was one of *the* Silverlights. My brother done take the stage all the way up there to see 'em. They never heard of you.'

'But,' Lance protested, his Lightning still in his hand but in no threatening manner. 'I *am* a Silverlight.'

'Yeah, thass right.' The broad-chested Bull had raised his voice even louder. 'They said the only

Silverlights they could think of would be a distant branch of the family, a bunch of feckless, razor-backed, barnyard savages with a morsel of sandy land along the Red who ain't never done no good. Those are the mongrels you're from, ain't you, mister? I oughta shoot you now and check the breed.'

Lance could not help but smile at this colourful description. 'Sounds like you got the gist of us. Good ole Quince. So you're behind this, are you? Never thought you'd be a snitch.'

Quince faced up to him alongside the brothers. 'I didn't say nuthin', Lance. You saved my skin once and I been grateful. But I can't go along with you on this. You better do as they say and clear out. Leave Marie alone.'

'Yeah? She's too good for me, is she? But not for you?' Lance clacked tight his revolver's newfangled swing-out cylinder. 'Perhaps me and this might think different. You with me, Pedro?'

'*Si, amigo.*' Pedro's hand slid to the butt of the ancient revolver holstered along his thigh. 'You are my friend so maybe I have to help you.'

'Yeah, not like this yellow rat turncoat who used to be our pard.'

'I terminated our partnership some time ago, if you remember,' Quince gritted out. 'I don't want trouble, Lance. Why don't you just go?'

'Because, my friends, I figure all your hot air is just bluff. To tell you the truth, I have no wish to kill you, Bull, or you Jack. Marie might not appreciate that. And I'm sure Pedro does not wish to blow you away, Quince. But you cut loose your dog we're going to be forced to. Ain't that so, Pedro?'

'*Si.*' The Mexican pushed back his chair from the table. 'It looks that way.'

'This time I'm warning you,' Bull blustered, aware that all the folks in the saloon were hanging on their words and backing away out of the firing line. 'Get outa this town and keep going. Your kinda scum ain't welcome in this vicinity.'

'Those are hard words, Bull. Nor do I take kindly to insults about my family' – now the Lighting was aimed at the big man's belt – 'so might I just inform you that if I wish to see your sister Marie, I will do so. I might even persuade her to elope with me. She's old enough to be married without your say-so.'

Bull stood his ground, his forefinger hooked around the trigger of the carbine as he held it waist high aimed towards Silverlight. 'You touch her and you die.'

'Yeah,' Jack put in, 'it's lucky for us we stepped in, in time 'fore a mongrel like you had his filthy way with her.'

'True.' Lance Silverlight batted his long lashes and gave his reckless grin. 'I reckon it is. You think so, eh? Listen, boys, and listen hard; I'll pay as much attention to you as I would to an empty bottle. We've got a half full one here to attend to, so why doncha all just blow? You're disturbin' me.'

The two Durhams stood staring at him like angry terriers. Quince's fingers toyed with the walnut butt of his old Colt. He swallowed hard, tense, but prepared to go the whole hog. He hoped against hope it wouldn't come to that. It could only be a bloodbath. It was so silent he could hear the ticking of the clock....

'You've been warned,' Bull roared. 'You've got 'til sundown. We see your face in Three Rivers again you're a dead man.' He clomped out of the saloon, followed by Jack and Quince, mounted up, and led them away at a brisk trot.

Lance was more het-up, his blood racing through him, than he cared to reveal. 'The nerve. You hear what they called me? Feckless.... razor-backed.... barnyard savage?'

'*Si*, I theenk half the town did.'

'This ain't no good.' Silverlight gasped as the tequila hit him. 'It ain't no good. No, suh. I ain't givin' her up. That gal's got to be mine.'

'But, *amigo*, just theenk; thees girl seem so sweet and innocent to you. With brothers like that, how can she be? Beware, one day she will show you her true colours. You try to get the saddle on her she will show you the white of her eye. She will keeck you in the *cojones*. Thass the way eet weel be.'

'You think so, my friend?' Lance rubbed his unshaven chin, perplexedly. 'Maybe you got a point. How could I live with a family like that?'

He sat for a while, chewing on a toothpick, as the rubberneckers lost interest and turned back to their card games. Then he beckoned Pedro closer and lowered his voice. 'Old Man Durham's got sixty or so fine horses in his corral. We could get a thousand dollars for them south of the border.'

'You crazy? You wanna steal them?'

'It's worth thinkin' about. It would sure teach

them braggarts a lesson. What say you?'

'Oh, I dunno,' One Eye demurred. 'Eet would be askin' for trouble.'

# FIVE

Old Man Durham sat in his big chair, with its curved wooden armrests, and glowered across the parlour table at his daughter Marie.

'Me and the boys gotta take a trip down to the Rio Grande to buy another thousand head of cattle from a Mex *ranchero*.' He used the back of his hand to wipe the breakfast remains from his heavy moustache. 'We'll be away a week or so. Until I get back you're gated, gal.'

'Oh,' Marie wailed. 'Can't I go to the barn dance?'

'You ain't goin' nowhere. You hear that, Mother? You keep her cooped up here tight as the hens in the hen house at nights. There's too many flea-bitten coyotes sneakin' around. She's on a tight leash.'

Olga Durham nodded. 'It's for your own good, Marie. We know what's best for you.'

'Yeah, we know what's best,' Bull agreed through a mouthful of oatcake. 'We see that lousy, no-good Silverlight sonuvabitch anywhere near this ranch he'll be one dead duck.'

'Filthy coward wouldn't dare,' young Jack sneered.

'We sceered the shit outa him. He'll be ridin' back fast as he can for the Red River, you betcha.'

'Boys,' their mother admonished, 'we don't want no barnyard language at the breakfast-table.'

'Yeah, well, it's true, ain't it?' Bull got up to reach for his carbine and shambled off outside, followed by his brother. 'We'll be saddling the hosses, Pa. How long we gonna be away?'

'Aw, a coupla days to ride down there, a couple to make the negotiations and to get the herd across the Grande, and a week's drive back here.'

When they had gone Durham eyed his daughter severely. 'When I get back, you and I will be going on a little trip, young lady. We'll be going by steamer from Corpus Christi up to Galveston and along to N'awleans. There's some wealthy merchants in that city. They ain't all uppity freed slaves dancin' in the streets. They have what they call salons where they mingle and meet. There's plenty of 'em will be lookin' out for a perty decent gal like you to marry one of their sons.'

'I don' want to go to N'awleans. I don't wanna marry no merchant's stuck-up son. Lance is the man I want, Pa. Doncha see, he ain't really a no-good drifter? He jest ain't had the opportunity to do well. He ain't had the guidance. Couldn't you help him, Pa, give him a start, a leg-up? I wish you would.'

Old Man Durham frowned at her mother. 'Once a river's set on its course there ain't no way of altering it, Marie. I've heard about this boy. He's a bad lot. There's no way he'll change.'

'He seemed a nice enough young fellow when he

came to tea,' Olga said, 'but he lied to us trying to make out his family was wealthy.'

'Yeah, he's a liar. And a liar never changes.'

'Most Texans are liars, ain't they, Pa? Allus tellin' tall tales. They're renowned for it.'

'That's different. That's just a bit of fun.' Durham cleared his throat, awkwardly. 'Another thing, if I don't fix you up in N'awleans, when you git back I'm enrollin' you in what they call a finishin' school up at Beaumont. You'll learn some manners there.'

'What?' Marie gave an irate screech. 'I don't want to go back to school. I'm not a kid.'

'You'll like it Marie,' her mother soothed. 'You'll study music, painting, poetry, fashion, how to behave like a proper young lady. It's gonna cost us.'

'We can afford it. Nuthin's too good for a Durham gal.'

'You've got your responsibilities to your family, Marie. You've got to make a proper match,' her mother reminded her. 'There'll be no running off with some low down, gun-slinging, saddle tramp. You want to be poor the rest of your life?'

'Poor ain't a good thing to be,' her father said, 'believe me.'

The girl stood, her lips compressed, and stalked out, without a word. The way she slammed the door summed up her feelings.

'She's sure taken a shine to this young stranger,' Olga mused. 'He's too handsome for his own good. Or hers.'

'Yep,' Durham sighed, 'we're gonna have to check her with a three-quarter rope and a snubbing post.

While I'm gone don't let that frolicsome filly outa your sight. She's too damn headstrong. Seems like you in that respect, if you remember, Olga.'

'Sure,' Olga smiled. 'You didn't have a cent when I met you and I married you aginst all advice.'

'Didn't have a cent? I was in hock up to my eyeballs.' Her husband laughed and got up to take a rifle from the rack. He kissed his wife goodbye. 'We'd better be headin' for the Grande. We need more stock to make the trip north worthwhile.'

Lance Silverlight had drifted back along the Neuces to Oakville and found at the post office there, as he had hoped, a letter from Marie. He sniffed at the perfume. 'Wouldja read this, please?' he asked the postmistress.

The woman slit it open and smiled. '*Dear Lance, I miss you so much* – ooh, whee! – *the touch of your hands and your kisses* – hey, you don't say?'

'Jest read it. No need for the interjections.';

'*I pray this reaches you, dear Lance* – hmm, dated two days ago – *as Daddy and the boys have gone south to buy more cows. They'll be gone a week, at least. The coast will be clear. Just give a whistle at midnight. Mama gets very tired and sleeps like a log. I'm longing to see you again, my darling. Come, if you can, please.*'

The postmistress ceased tracing a finger along the lines and grinned at him. 'While the cat's away, eh? Well, ain't you the lucky lover boy?'

'Ain't there anythang else?'

'Only *All my love and kisses, Marie*. How much more you want there to be? The gal's got the hots for you.'

He snatched the flimsy sheet and kissed it. 'Come on, Pedro. You see! She loves me.'

'Hang on, *amigo*. We already got one lynch party lookin' for us,' Pedro hissed. 'You want to double that? I say we get out now, go to Mexico. Let things cool off.'

'Aw, we can give them all the slip. I gotta go see Marie.' Silverlight suddenly realized the post lady was listening. 'You won't repeat this?'

'Hell no. Young love. It's wonderful. If only I'd met a fella like you when I was a gal. Go, boy, go see her.'

'Pliz, no, don' encourage him,' Pedro begged. 'He crazy enough already.'

'Hot damn. Me and Marie, we'll elope down to Mexico. That's what we'll do. Once we're wed her ole man'll be bound to come round. He'll cough up the dowry, sure enough.'

'*Si*, with his rifle.' Pedro shrugged, exasperatedly, at the woman. 'You see?'

'Come on, Pedro. What you waiting for? Let's ride. *Vamos, amigo.*'

'Golly gee!' Marie sighed as, that night, she stretched out on the bed of straw in the barn. 'I do declare, I thought you was goin' to set the hay alight the way you been lovin' me, so hard, so fast.'

'Yeah.' Lance Silverlight collapsed exhausted beside her, sweat runnelling down his bare chest. 'That ain't nuthin' to the way I'm goin' to love you down in Mexico.'

'Mexico,' she repeated, softly, threading her

fingers through his. 'What you talkin' about, Lance?'

'Mexico. That's where we got to go, Marie. While your ol' man's away. We're going to elope tonight.'

'Elope? You mean we'll go down there and git married and come back 'fore he gets home?'

'No .... that wouldn't be a good idea. Him and them brothers of yours would most likely pepper me on the spot they'd be so mad. I mean we'll elope. We'll live down there.'

'In Mexico?' Marie's voice rose in a wail of disbelief. 'What we wanna live in Mexico for? They're all dirt poor down there.'

'It ain't so bad. It's a great place, so free and easy. We'll have a ball. And, fer hell's sake, I gotta go. There's a damn posse of lynchers after me.'

'Lynchers?'

'Yeah. Why you keep repeatin' everythang? You creep back in the house, Marie. Hurry, it's getting late. Just pack a few necessities in a bag and we'll hightail it outa here.'

'Hightail it?'

'Yes. You can ride a hoss, cain't ya?'

'I can, but, Lance, I'm s'posed to be goin' to ladies' college. What'll I say to Mama?'

'You don't tell her nuthin'. Don't wake her. What's the matter with you, Marie? We're going to elope. You comin' or not?'

'Lance, I just can't run out like that. I mean, what would we do in Mexico? It's a horrible place, full of bandits and tarantula spiders and everybody's shooting everybody all the time, or else they're starving. I don't wanna go to Mexico, Lance.'

'You ain't coming?'

'I love you, Lance.' She stared at him, distraught, as he jumped to his feet, pulling on his black shirt. 'But I can't go to Mexico. Why's anybody want to lynch you?'

'Why the hell you think? Aw, Jeesis! Hot damn. So this is what you call love? You mustn't leave your mammy's side?' He buckled on his gunbelt, swinging the revolver to hang behind his right hip. 'For the last time, are you coming or not?'

Marie started sobbing. 'I can't, Lance. Not just like that.'

'Shee-it!' He kicked a bucket clanging against the barn wall. 'What you scared of? Them pig-eyed brothers of yourn? Your bull-headed old man?'

'What the hell's going on?' A voice yelled from over at the house. 'Is that you, Marie? What you doing out of bed?'

'Aw, no!' Lance peered out of the barn door through the darkness and saw her mother hanging out of her bedroom window, rags in her hair, and in her flannel nightie. 'That's all we need.'

'Please, Lance,' Marie caught hold of him as he buttoned his pants. 'Please don't go to Mexico.'

'I've got to go, Marie.' He stared into her wild eyes. Funny how the intensity of passion that he had felt for four hours as he made love to his *amor* should suddenly turn into virulent anger. 'Let me go!' He pushed her away roughly. 'I've had enough of you and your whole damn family. I'll tell you what I'm goin' to do. I'm leavin' and I'm taking your hosses with me.'

'Our horses?'

'Yeah, all of 'em.'

'But, why, Lance? That won't solve anything.'

'Why? I'll tell you why.' He pointed a finger at her face. 'Your old man won't let me marry you unless I'm rich. So I'm goin' to git rich and to start me off, I'm taking his remuda. He's gonna help me up the ladder even if he don't like it.'

'Lance, he needs those horses for the cattle drive. He'll come after you with the boys. He'll kill you.'

'He can try.' Angrily, Lance tossed his dark hair, crammed his hat on his head, pulled on his leather topcoat. 'But you tell him, if he does, I ain't going to be aiming to miss.'

'Who's that over there?' A cowboy yelled from the bunkhouse, one of the skeleton crew left to tend the herd in the Durhams' absence. 'Come outa there with your hands high or I'm going to start shooting.'

For reply, Silverlight put two fingers to his lips and gave a piercing whistle. Out in the corral Pedro heard it and, opening the gate, began yipping at the big herd of mustangs, using his lariat as a whip. They didn't need much urging and went pushing and jumping out of there, and in one great flowing movement headed away across the plain, setting the cattle stampeding.

'I'm coming out gun smoking,' Lance shouted, pulling his Lightning. At the barn door he turned and stared at the girl. 'I'm sorry, Marie. A man with no money's no right fallin' in love. One day I'll be back. You wait for me.'

The rustler ran out, crouching low, firing at the

men who were coming from the bunkhouse door. He aimed low and the one who had challenged him gave a cry, 'Agh!' He crumpled, a bullet through the flesh of his thigh. Two others jumped over him and started crashing out shots, wildly, as Silverlight raced to the corral and leapt on Beater. He whipped the loose-tied rein free and, spurring him, set off after One Eye Pedro and the horses who were fast disappearing into the night.

'Stop him!' Mrs Durham shouted. 'Get him. Shoot the bastard.'

As the two cowhands ran to find a horse only to discover there were none left for them, the lady of the house looked down at her daughter, Marie, who was standing in the yard, her dress rumpled, straw clinging to her hair, staring vainly after her departed lover.

'Marie, git your ass up here,' she bellowed. 'What in hell's going on? I hope you got a good explanation.'

'Keep them cattle moving,' Old Man Durham roared as he watched his herd of more than a thousand longhorns being swum across the Rio Grande.

The river was nearly 200 yards wide at this point, a cattle ford known as Paso Ganado, six miles below Fort Brown and no more than thirty miles from the Gulf. There was very little current but it was deep and needed swimming from bank to bank. His son, Bull, was leading the first batch of 200 head, the cattle, noses raised and horns tossing, instinctively following him urged on by shrill cries of Mexican *vaqueros* swimming their mustangs from the opposite bank.

When they reached the middle of the river the Mexicans turned back to cut out the next bunch of 200. It was Quince's turn to plunge Feathers into the water. He had chosen her for the broadness of her 'bread basket', an indicator of a good swimmer, and she proved just that, pushing her way across like a streamlined duck. Quince had cast aside his boots and all he had to do was hang on to the scruff of her mane and let her go.

Bull yelled at him as they passed, 'Them *vaqueros* don't waste much time. They'll have the next batch ready by the time you're across.' When he had completed the strenuous swim and his horse lurched up the bank, he shouted to Old Man Durham, 'They're coming fast and furious. It won't take long now.'

His father had no time to converse with him because he was busy trying to count the cattle as they came struggling out of the river and scrambling up the bank. He did so by using a tally string on which were ten knots, slipping a knot through his fingers for every ten beasts, and when a hundred had passed going back down the string to count the next hundred.

Across the gully through which the herd was being urged by John Durham's Circle Dot cowboys, was the Mexican *caporal* who was making his own count. His method was to have ten pebbles and pass one pebble to his other hand for every ten longhorns, and so on, back again.

When all the cattle were across and the count

completed, Old Man Durham called out, 'I made it one thousand and thirty-five.' The Mexican was one under, and the Custom House man, who had ridden out to keep an eye on the transaction, was one over. So they settled for Durham's count.

The seller, Don Luis Arroyo, arrayed in silver-decorated tight black velvet, and in one of the biggest sombreros Bull had ever seen, weighted down with silver conchos, rode up on a high-stepping stallion, its harness and saddle adorned with even more silver. '*Bueno*,' he called in Spanish. 'You satisfied, *señor?*'

Old Man Durham sure was, for the long-legged, pale-coloured southern cattle were in good flesh for such an early season of the year. He was garbed without pretension in a dusty suit, big bandanna and high-crowned Stetson, looking much like any other of his cowboys. He tried to conceal his satisfaction, giving a nod and a grunt, and sticking out a horny hand to seal the deal.

Don Luis invited him, by means of an interpreter, to ride into the bank at Brownsville and make payment in gold, after which he would host a dinner for the American cattleman at the town hotel.

'You boys get the herd moving,' Durham told Bull. 'You oughta be able to make five miles by nightfall. I guess I'll stay the night in town. You know how these Mexes like to take their time over everything. Start 'em moving first light and I'll catch up with you.'

Before departing, he rode over to Quince, his new wrangler, whose job would be to drive thirty newly bought horses in their remuda. 'Have the boys cast lots for the hosses of their choice and make sure they use 'em equally. I don't want some ruined. You'll be needing all the horses you got on the long trail north.'

Still, with the sixty in the coral at his home, John Durham figured they would have sufficient for the job. He watched the herd move away in natural snaking formation northwards, the chuck wagon, hauled by four mules, jangling along on one side. He felt mighty pleased with the transaction and rode off to join Don Luis and his bodyguards. He would now have more than 2000 good cattle to send up the trail.

At Brownsville he had the bank pay out Don Luis. The two 'barons of beef' were enjoying as fine a meal as could be provided at Brown's Hotel, followed by cigars and brandy, when Bull came racing down the street in a dust cloud, leaping from his mount, stomping up on to the sidewalk and bursting into the hotel. 'Pa,' he cried, flush-faced and almost choking with anger. 'We been robbed of the horses.'

Durham gawped at him, open-mouthed. 'What horses?'

'The horses at home, at the ranch. The whole remuda. That bastard. I'll kill him. He stampeded the herd, too, with the shooting.'

'Shooting? What shooting? Who?'

'That Lance Silverlight, the mongrel who's been sniffing around Marie. Sam Strange has just arrived with the news. He rode sixty miles a day to get to us. Him and his hoss are just about done in.'

'OK, calm down.' John Durham had got to his feet, his wrinkled cheeks turning a fiery colour, and it wasn't just the brandy. 'Was anybody hurt? Are your ma and Marie all right?'

'Yeah, I think so. It's all Marie's fault for encouraging that slimy snake's advances. Apparently they've been meeting secretly out in the barn right under our noses. Bob Flood was shot in the leg but he should be OK.'

'How's the herd?'

'Waal, only the boys on night herd had a hoss to go after it. I told you, he stole the whole damn remuda we had ready for the trail. With nobody to turn 'em I figure the stampede would run for ten miles 'fore they slowed. They could be scattered all over the plain.'

John Durham slowly shook his head as the news sank in. 'I knew that varmint was trouble. The worthless, useless son of a bitch. I thought you said you'd run him out of town.'

'I thought we had, too. Apparently he was with that Mex side-kick of his, One Eye Pedro.'

'You should have killed him, killed them both.'

'I wish we had. I really wish I'd blown him to Kingdom Come, or t'other place, like I wanted to.'

'Who is this man?' Don Luis asked.

'Huh, he's a stinkin' piece of offal who don't deserve to live,' John Durham roared. 'Lance Silverlight's his handle. He's no more than nineteen. Sees himself as a fancy shootist and a ladies' man, all snazzily duded out in black leather. He's riding for a fall. You ever come across him, Don Luis, I'll pay handsomely for his capture. Bring him to me alive. I want to see him hanged.'

'How handsomely, *amigo*?'

'How—?'

'*Si*, how much price you put on his head? Would it be worth our trouble?'

'Five hundred dollars. That's what I would pay to see him die.'

Don Luis smiled, craftily. 'That is very interesting,' he said, through his interpreter. 'We will have to look out for this boy.'

# SIX

Lance Silverlight woke with a start, jerking the Lightning from his holster. There was little light from their camp-fire and he shivered as the ghostly shape of a long-eared owl swooped low. 'I'm gittin' the spooks,' he muttered and tossed a log making sparks flare up.

'What's wrong, *amigo?*' Pedro sat up, pulling his poncho around him for it got cold at nights.

'Nuthin'. Just a damn hooty owl woke me. No wonder the Comanch' think they're bad luck. Give me the creeps.' He blew dust from the cylinder of the revolver. It was his pride and joy. 'Heat up some coffee, Pedro, ole pal.' As the Mexican built up their fire and did so, Silverlight dug out a tin of melted tallow and used a rag to lubricate the handgun and the bullets he inserted. The Lightning was Colt's first double action. Previously they had thought self-cockers wasteful of ammunition and inaccurate. But the previous year, 1881, they had brought out this six-shooter which they claimed to be the fastest there was . . . 'exceeding in accuracy and penetration any other pistol'.

'I've only killed two men yet,' he said, 'but if I'm forced to add to my score this is the weapon that'll do it.' He glanced along at the roped-in remuda of stolen horses. 'Those babies are worth all of a thousand dollars. We need to get rid of 'em but I ain't letting them go for a fraction of that to some greaser, if you'll pardon the epithet.'

'OK, *gringo*, but, if so, we better get moving for there ain't nobody in these parts with more than a few pesos in his pockets. If we don't sell them soon they might be extracted from us forcibly. We are in *bandido* country.'

'Yeah. I was wonderin' why I'd developed a bad case of the shakes since we swam the Rio Grande.'

It had been no easy job driving the remuda of sixty horses, a job normally requiring four or five skilled riders. Pedro had led the way, guiding the flow of whinnying mustangs at a fierce lope, dropping back to whip in with his lariat-end any who tried to quit the bunch, but the herd instinct was strong and not many made a break for freedom.

Lance had to keep his bandanna high and his eyes narrowed behind his sunglasses against the cloud of choking dust kicked up by 120 pairs of hoofs as he chased them along, whooping and cursing as he urged them on across the plain.

They had put a good distance between themselves and the Durham ranch, without any trouble or pursuit – they would be too busy rounding up their cows. Pedro wanted to carry on along the Neuces westwards towards Eagle Pass, reach the state of Coahuila.

Silverlight had disagreed. 'That's what they'll expect us to do. I say go south, skirt Laredo, and cross the Grande at San Ignacio north of Falcon

Lake. Then we can head for Monterrey. There's plenty of rich Mexican ranchers in the state of Nuevo Leon would be glad to give us a fair price.'

He won the decision on the toss of a silver dollar. 'It's up to you, *amigo*,' Pedro grumbled. 'There might be more *rancheros* but there are also many more *rurales*.'

'So?' Lance grinned. 'They will protect us from *bandidos*, won't they?'

'If they don't hang us.'

The Circle Dot brand used by the Santa Esmeralda ranch was pretty easy to disguise. They simply used a red hot running iron to turn it into the 'Wagon Wheel' outfit. Well, that was the easy part. First they had to catch and drag each individual horse over to their fire. It took them all of one day. It didn't help that hazy low cloud had created a sweltering heat that numbed their minds and made their shirts stick to their backs.

They were more than glad when they reached the Rio Grande. Beater took to the water like a turtle. A swimming horse needs freedom and Lance scarcely touched the reins; just giving gentle slaps on the neck, he guided his horse for the far shore. Behind him Pedro sent the herd swimming and splashing after them. They only lost one horse who suddenly sank like a stone. Nor did he reappear, although they watched out for him.

'That's real weird,' Lance remarked, as he emptied the river water from his boots. 'He musta got the cramps.'

They had unsaddled their own broncs and allowed

them to roll in the damp sand. Then they headed on into Mexico.

Now, by the light of their fire, they supped at tin cups of scalding black coffee, as Lance examined his boots with their emblazoned silver 'Lone Star' of Texas. 'These cost me sixty dollars, hand-sewn, to my own design,' he said. 'It's being a snappy dresser gets the gals.'

'You still theenkin' of your li'l chickadee?'

'Marie? Damn right, I am. That gal got me with a centre shot, Pedro. I ain't gonna fergit her in a hurry. What a damn fool thang to do. Of all the horses in Texas why did I have to steal her daddy's. I jest saw red, I guess. I figured he owed me somethang. I tell you, Pedro, I got a sinkin' feelin' that when I done that I dug my own grave.'

'Hey, *caramba*! Cheer up, *amigo*. You just homeseck. In Mexico there plenty more chickadees, you'll see.'

'Yeah, I guess it's this graveyard hour' – the still, cold, thick darkness when the night seems endless, was, he thought, probably making him feel morbid, but he couldn't shake the feeling off. 'Nobody worries about a bit of small-time rustling for long. Hell, it's the second occupation of most Texans. But large scale horse-thievery from a rich, well-known rancher? This they ain't gonna forget. This puts us beyond the pale. We're wanted outlaws now, Pedro, with a price on our heads. Maybe this time we bit off more than we can chew.'

'Well, *hombre*, I hate to say so but it was your idea.'

Lance clacked the Lightning's cylinder home, spun the revolver on one finger, and grinned across at Pedro. 'Look after your Colt and your Colt will look after you. Thass what they say. Let's pray it proves true. Though I ain't so sure about that ancient cap'n ball smoke-pole you carry. Maybe you should update yourself.'

'Less hope that ain't necessary. We ain't come to Mexico to start a war. Soon as we sell these hosses I go see my family.' Pedro jumped to his feet. 'Come on, I see a glimmer of dawn on the horizon. Let's be going. It not far to Los Herrerras. There's a rich *haciendado* lives there. We do business with him, maybe?'

'What's his name?'

'Don Luis Arroyo.'

'Right. Let's go.'

Old Man Durham stomped into his ranch house followed by his two sons, Bull and Jack. They all glowered at Marie, who was laying table for dinner, but did not greet her. 'You're just in time,' Olga Durham called, bearing in a steaming dish of potatoes. 'Have you all washed up?'

When they were seated, John Durham carved the boiled ham and passed plates around. 'A man afoot's useless,' he growled.

'What do you mean, John?'

'What do I mean?' He hammered his knife handle so loud on the table Marie visibly jumped. 'What you think I mean, Olga? We got a herd of two thousand beeves waiting to go north and we don't have the horses. That's what I mean.'

'Didn't you have any luck buying any?'

'Luck?' Bull jeered. 'We don't have much luck with *her* around.'

'Bull, don't talk about your sister like that,' Olga chided. 'She—'

'She's the cause of our damn troubles,' Jack cut in. 'That's what she is.'

'Strangely enough, Mother,' the Old Man explained, 'it's harder to find good horses in this part of Texas than to find a gold mine. We must have rode fifty miles today and all we've come back with are three. The other ranchers are taking their herds up the trail. They need all the horses they've got. They're laughing at me behind my back because they know they'll be first in Kansas and get the best price.'

'You've got thirty new ones spare in the corral, thirty-three now,' Olga said. 'Isn't that enough?'

'No, it isn't enough, woman,' the Old man shouted, staring angrily at his wife. 'We need at least another forty.'

'No need to take that tone, John.'

'It ain't Ma's fault, Pa.'

'All right, go on, say it,' Marie blurted out. 'Over and over again. It's my fault. How can it be my fault? I didn't know he was going to take the horses.'

'You knew he was a no-good drifter,' Bull shouted. 'It was you had that lousy snake sneak in here.'

'All right, that's enough,' the Old Man said, trying to placate his wife. 'Pass them black-eye beans, Bull. Don't hog 'em all yourself. Anyone want any more ham? It's real tasty.'

'How long am I to be treated like a leper?' Marie asked. 'How long you going to go on not speaking to me?'

'You'll find out soon enough, Daughter. There ain't gonna be no trip to N'awleans. There ain't gonna be no fancy ladies' college, neither. In the morning you and I are taking a trip down river to Corpus Christi.'

'Corpus Christi?' Marie was startled. 'What for?'

'You'll find out what for. You heard of that convent at Orange Grove?'

'Convent? I don't wanna go to no convent? I don't wanna be a nun.'

'You ain't gonna be a nun,' her father said. 'You'll just live there for at least four months this summer. I want to know you're under lock and key and out of harm's way. I can't trust you to behave decent on your own. The nuns will teach you how to behave, how to control them urges of yourn. There'll be no smuggling lonesome cowboys into your room down there.'

'Please, Pa.' Tears began to roll down Marie's cheeks. 'I'll behave. I'll never go out with another boy. Please don't send me to the nuns, Pa.'

'It's all settled. If you were a boy I'd have larruped the sin outa you with my belt. But I gotta let the nuns do it.'

'It's for your own good, Marie,' her mother soothed. 'Otherwise you're just going to go to hell and damnation. You gotta learn the meaning of Christianity.'

'Aw, tell her to quit that sobbing, Ma,' Bull said. 'I cain't abide a wailing woman.'

'You!' Marie suddenly jumped to her feet. 'I hate you all. If you'd been nicer to Lance, if you'd let me marry him, none of this would have happened. No, you had to run him out of town. No wonder he got angry. Oh, yes, I hate you all. I wish I'd gone with him.'

They sat in surprised silence as the girl ran from the room, slamming the door, listened to her sobbing as she climbed the stairs to her room. 'First thing in the morning you have her bag packed, Mother, ready to go. I'll take the buggy,' John Durham said. 'She's got to learn.'

'You know, Pa,' Bull Durham said, between shovelling back mouthfuls of food again. 'I reckon some of them ranchers wouldn't sell us their horses because you fought on the Union side. Folks around here don't forget.'

'Yuh,' the Old Man grunted. 'Maybe.'

Quince was over at the corral coiling his lariat preparing to make a throw at the head of one of the three new mustangs. He had been badly treated and as a result had a nasty nature, a kicker and biter, spooked by the slightest movement. He needed to be gentled. The wrangler, unlike most others, believed a horse responded to kindness, not cruelty. But it was going to take some time to win this one round. However, it was his job to have every mount ready and rideable, so he had gone out to the corral after chow to see what he could do.

'Nice work, boy.' The Old Man had strolled across to watch him handle the horse. He admired the way he cut him out, pacified him, and gently eased himself on his back. The mustang had set off, leaping and bucking, putting air between Quince's pants and the saddle, but he stayed on and gradually slowed him to a trotting pace. 'I wouldn't have bought that 'un, but it was a case of all I could get. Bring him over here, I wanna talk to you.'

'What is it, Mr Durham?'

'How you feel about the theft of our remuda?'

'I'm damn hopping mad, like I expect you are, too.'

'I'm livid, boy. But I can't spare the men to go after that sneakin' coyote. Anyhow, I guess he's well away by now. He was a friend of yourn, wasn't he?'

'*Was* is the word, Mr Durham. When we were kids. But not now. No more.'

'He's fast with a gun, ain't he?'

'True. Deadly as a rattler when he strikes.'

'Would you be sceered of comin' up agin him?'

'I guess I would. But I'd be ready to.'

'Good, 'cause I want you to go after him.'

'On my own?'

'I know it ain't ideal. But, like I said, I can't spare nobody to side you. This is just a suggestion, Quince. I won't blame you if you refuse an' we'll say no more about it. But if you bring that buzzard back alive there'll be five hundred dollars for you.'

'Five hundred?' Quince circled around on the skittish mustang. 'Are you serious? That's big money.'

'It's a big job. I aim to hang Silverlight so I got to pay for that pleasure.'

'Cain't see much pleasure in a hanging. But I guess you're right. Lance laid down the gauntlet. He knows the penalty if he loses.' Quince slipped the noose from the horse's neck and jumped lightly to the ground, setting him free. He met Durham's eyes. 'It could well be me who loses. Hell, I'll do it. When do I start?'

'Tonight. You got any cash?'

'Not 'til pay day.'

'Here's your thirty dollars in advance. Remember, if you *can*, bring him back alive. But, if you can't, kill him.'

Quince slipped the silver dollars into his pocket. 'This has got a nasty taste to it, bein' a hired killer.'

'You ain't doin' it just for the reward. You'll be acting out of loyalty to this ranch, your own stubborn pride, and you'll be upholding the unwritten law of Texas.'

'I will?' Quince grinned at his employer. 'If you put it like that it sure makes me feel better.'

He gave a whistle to Feathers, who obediently trotted across, always ready for an outing. Quince slung his saddle over his back. 'We're goin' some place we never been, ole pal, south of the border, down Mexico way, 'cause I figure that's where he musta headed.'

'Come in the house and git a carbine an' a coupla boxes of slugs. Don't say nuthin' to the others about this or they'll wanna go, too. I'll have my wife fix you up with grub for a few days. Then you'll be on your own.' The rancher's eyes were stone steady as he offered his hand and gripped the youth's. 'Good luck, boy.'

'Yep. I figure I'll be needin' some.'

Don Luis Arroyo's powerful stallion, which he was proud to call the finest horse in the state of Nuevo Leon, was restrained by cruel harnessing, a spade bit with a sharp raised plate that lay across the beast's tongue, silver curbs under the jaw to control him, and a peculiar spiked contraption about his lower parts that deterred him from attempting to mount a mare, a sort of reverse chastity belt. Don Luis rode deep in his heavy, decorated saddle, its tapaderas, or fenders, protecting the black velveteen of his flared trousers against the vicious cacti and thorn scrub of the baking plateau he and his cohort of riders were traversing.

He was pleased with the deal he had done with the Yankee rancher, and with the pouches of solid gold coin in his saddle-bags. He crossed the river to Matamoros, followed its southern bank to Rio Bravo and Reynosa, then set off across the parched lands until they reached the San Juan valley and headed for Los Herrerras.

Although neither party for the moment realized it, Silverlight and Pedro from the north, and Don Luis from the south, were converging in a pincer movement, crossing the don's vast lands to his fortified hacienda. Such space was necessary to support his cattle for each longhorn needs at least twenty acres to graze so sparse was the feeding.

The building, itself, was a high-walled and turreted former Spanish mission confiscated from the church by Juarez, the Indian, who had ruled Mexico for several years with his crazy idealistic ideas about dividing the land among the *peons*, with free education and medical care, shooting priests and disinheriting the big landowners.

But now he was dead and Porfirio Diaz had seized power, ruling Mexico with an iron fist through his tentacles of armed *federales* and *rurales*. From his palace in Mexico City, Diaz had rewarded Don Luis with this great house and its lands alongside a fertile river valley for his loyal support through the troubled years. So there he lived like a feudal lord.

However, Mexico was rarely free of trouble and there was rumour of another revolution brewing in these barren northern states. The haughty Don Luis

Arroyo, in his reports to *El Presidente*, dismissed these ragged-trousered discontents as mere bandit scum. 'They pose no threat to the rule of law and order,' he had informed Diaz. But he was not so sure. There was rumour that they were receiving modern weapons from north of the border. If they made contact with revolutionaries in the south there could be danger. 'I will be vigilant and do all in my power to aid the governor in stamping out any insurrection,' he wrote. 'May I assume I have your excellency's permission to use such methods as I see fit?'

In other words, imprisonment, interrogation under torture, arbitrary execution, hanging, shooting, burning of villages suspected of harbouring terrorists.

Not that Don Luis was an overly cruel man. He prided himself on his largesse to his workers, allowing them their fiestas, attending their weddings, sometimes, true, to take first taste of the bride, but it was an ancient custom. No, he was a sophisticated, educated man. He had to agree reluctantly that such methods were the norm and necessary to keep the *peons* in their place and Diaz balanced on top of his pyramid of power.

As he and his bunch of *vaqueros* approached the hacienda, a bell in one of the towers was tolled in greeting.

Those toiling in his fields turned to take off their hats and bow low to him as he rode by. The great oak gates were opened and he and his horsemen went sweeping through into a fountained courtyard, an oasis of palms and pleasantness. Don Luis swung down, tossing his reins to a groom. To the rear of the building was a more public courtyard, with stables, workshops, and the kitchens. But here at the front was the arched entranceway to his own apartments, banqueting hall and private chapel.

Don Luis's viciously spiked silver spurs jingled as he entered the blessedly cool and shadowy hall, with its vast fireplace, long polished table and carved chairs. He threw off his huge sombrero to reveal a mane of grey-flecked hair and a Castilian cast of features, the deeply grooved face of a man in his mid-fifties. A man in his prime, he would claim.

Two serving girls fluttered around, placing trays of sweetmeats on the table before him, pouring wine, brushing the dust from his costume. 'Don't fuss!' He seated himself, as Teresa, another girl of about fifteen, came forward to greet him.

'Ah, my dear.' He caught hold of her and pulled her by her slim waist on to one of his bony knees, kissing her lips. 'We had a successful trip. You, I trust, have been saying prayers for me.'

'*Si, señor.*' The black-haired, dark-eyed girl stiffened slightly against his embrace. She was not yet used to his caresses, his masculine smell of sweat and horses, his rough unshaven jaw. 'I pray every day for your safety.'

'Hm? I wonder?' Don Luis spoke in a deep guttural tone as he examined some documents that had arrived for him. 'You are a quiet one. Sometimes I wonder just what you are thinking.'

'I think only of you, *señor.*' Teresa came from a middle-class family, her father a lawyer in Monterrey.

She had somehow caught Don Luis's eye and had been shocked when he began to pay court to her. Even more shocked when this middle-aged grandee proposed not marriage, but that she should become his concubine. She was a virgin; she was in love with a young man, another lawyer; she protested and pleaded with her parents, but she suspected they had been bribed, or were in a state of fear. They made no protest when Don Luis Arroyo's men came and took her away. She had been horrified, disgusted, by the things he had done to her. But it was a *fait accompli* now. She had to accept the position with as much dignity as she could. One day, she suspected, she would fall out of favour and he would toss her away. Teresa forced herself to stroke his horny hand.

'Is there anything you need, *señor*?'

'Not for just now.' He glanced at her, smiling craftily, and lit a cigar. 'I wish you wouldn't call me *señor*. It is so formal, as if you are a servant girl. Just say Luis.'

'But I am your servant.' A sudden haughtiness showed itself in her delicately rounded face, the jut of her chin. 'What else am I?'

'Don't be a silly girl. No letter from the president? Ah, well, as they say, no news is good news.' He gave her a squeeze. 'How are you? Smile. Say something. Tonight we will have a great feast to celebrate my homecoming.'

An hour or so later he was dozing on his four-poster bed beside Teresa after some energetic love-making; that is, on his side, she barely responded; but she was shy, it was early days yet. Suddenly the tower bell began to toll, and, going to the window, he looked out across the plain. 'Who in heaven is this?' he asked.

A huge herd of horses was galloping towards the hacienda being urged on by what looked like two strangers, one a *gringo*, the other a Mexican. His *vaqueros* were riding to greet them with harsh cries and levelled rifles, surrounding them and guiding the flow of horseflesh into one of Don Luis Arroyo's corrals.

The middle-aged *aristo* watched the horses milling around and the two men being escorted towards the house. He pulled on his velveteen pants, boots and white, ruffled shirt, tied a crimson sash around his waist, and left the girl, to descend a spiral staircase to the banqueting hall. The dusty pair were being escorted in, none too gently it had to be admitted, by the don's leather-clad foreman, Enrique, and another guard.

Lance Silverlight shrugged away the foreman's restraining hand and asked, 'Is this how you greet an *Americano* who has ridden all this way to sell you fine horses?'

'Remove your hat,' Enrique snarled, 'when you speak to Don Luis.'

'Sure thang, your majesty,' Lance replied, with a grin, tossing it on to the table, pulling off his black gloves for good measure.

'*And* those curious spectacles. I like to see a man's eyes when he speaks to me.'

Silverlight did as he was bid, tucking the dark glasses into a shirt pocket, while Pedro, hat in hands, deemed it best to remain silent. 'I hear tell you're a fair businessman who buys and sells cattle and horses,' the Texan said. 'So that's why we've brought these to you. If you ain't interested we'll go on our way.'

'I doubt it.' Don Luis smiled in a knowing way. 'What brand is on these horses?'

'The Wagon Wheel ranch north of Laredo,' Silverlight interjected before the foreman could reply. 'We paid nine hundred dollars for 'em and we're willing to sell 'em to you for a thousand to cover our trouble.'

'I doubt it once again.'

'You doubt what, mister?'

'I doubt very strongly whether you paid a single cent for this stock.'

'All the brands have been recently tampered with,' Enrique said, in Spanish. 'It looks very much like not long ago they bore the brand of that *Americano*, the Circle Dot.'

'A rather childish attempt to hoodwink me, don't you think?'

'*Senor*,' Pedro began, 'we buy this stock in good faith from a man—'

'Shut up, dog.' His burly guard cuffed him across the jaw. 'Speak when you are spoken to.'

'Hey,' Lance protested, 'is this your idea of hospitality? Come on, Pedro, we're leaving.'

His hand had moved to the big Colt on his hip, half-easing it from the holster, trying to back away. But he was dissuaded by the carbine barrel held by Enrique to his head.

'You are going nowhere,' Don Luis snapped. 'Unless I say so. You stole those horses from my friend, John Durham. You fools, he, himself, told me so only four days ago. He asked me to be on the lookout for you. How kind of you to save us the bother. What an irony of fate that you present yourselves at my door.'

'Aw, shee-it!' Lance drawled, despondently. 'What a hell of a country. We ain't seen a soul in a hundred miles and the first one has to be you. Don't s'pose your honour could spare a glass of that wine? I'm parched and it looks mighty appetizing.'

His attention was distracted by the sight of a young, beautiful girl, her hair hanging loose, barefoot, holding a skimpy white dress together at her throat, who had descended the stairs and was standing watching. 'Howdy.' He flashed his lecherous, white-toothed smile. 'You the lady of the house? Pleased to meetcha.'

Enrique was about to club him with his carbine butt for his insolence, but Don Luis raised a hand. 'Teresa, give my guests a glass of wine. Let us show the *gringo* that we here in Mexico have civilized manners.'

The girl stole forward and nervously did as she was told. 'Who are they?' she asked.

'Two horse-thieves. But they have done me a favour so I will not be too harsh with them. John Durham should pay me well for such fine horses.'

Lance almost choked on his wine. 'You,' he spluttered, 'it's you who are the friggin' thieves.'

'That is not a polite thing to say, Señor Silversmith, is it?'

'Silverlight. Lance Silverlight. So what are you

gonna do with us, your high and mighty?'

This time Enrique did club him, swiftly and viciously, knocking the youth to his knees. Lance shook the hair from his eyes, winced, and regained his feet. He eyed the foreman who stood malevolently, his face like carved mahogany. 'I'll remember you,' he whispered.

For reply, Enrique gun-butted him again, swiftly, in the gut and he went down on one knee. 'So,' he asked, 'what are you planning to do, apart from beat the shit outa me?'

Don Luis smiled in his superior manner. 'John Durham has promised a good reward for your capture. We will return you to Texas. It will be a pleasure to watch them hang you.'

'In that case,' Silverlight drawled, getting a grip on the table to haul himself up, meeting the girl's concerned eyes, 'I might as well have another glass of that wine.'

'Here,' Don Luis said, pouring a glass. 'Let me help you.' He tossed it in the Texan's face. 'Take these scum away.'

# SEVEN

'Well, I'll be a monkey's uncle.' John Durham studied the telegram that had arrived over the wire from Brownsville. 'Take a squint at this. Don Luis has saved our bacon.'

SIXTY EXCELLENT HORSES AVAILABLE STOP MEET ME MATAMOROS IN THREE DAYS STOP PAYMENT THOUSAND DOLLARS IN GOLD STOP DON LUIS

Bull Durham slowly read out the message. 'There's something fishy about this, Pa. Why's he want to meet us his side of the river?'

His brother Jack snatched the cable. 'A thousand in gold. Can we afford that, Pa?'

'It's a case of having to. If they're sound horses it's a fair price. The sooner you get these cows to Dodge the sooner we'll have plenty more cash under the bed. C'mon, saddle up. We got a long ride.'

Unlike many of the richer Texan cattle barons who had greedily seized land until they had huge tracts much larger than they could handle, John Durham was a cautious man. He had hated using credit, even before the recent collapse of the banks and the subsequent slump. He, like Don Luis, preferred solid gold to paper money. Many of the big cattlemen had gone bust due to their folly or had sold out to foreign investors, mainly Scots, who were cannily parsimonious in their running of the spreads. Durham signed a deal not on paper but with a handshake. His word was his bond. He expected that of a 'gentleman' like Don Luis Arroyo to be the same.

He could not chance leaving his big herd untended, so only he and his two sons rode south, not expecting trouble. They reached Brownsville in good time and swam their broncs across the Rio Grande on the third day. A group of Mexicans and the herd of sixty horses was waiting for them outside Matamoros.

'He's got a damn helluva lot of *vaqueros* with him,' Bull growled, as they approached. 'He don't need all them to drive a pack of hosses.'

'Yeah,' Jack muttered, 'an' they're all armed to the teeth.'

John Durham tugged his battered Stetson down over his weatherbeaten face and rode forward to a tall, dark-faced Mexican he recognized as Don Luis's *segundo*.

'Greetings, *señor*, my master cannot be with us. He has other important business.' Enrique gave a yellow-toothed grin as his men gathered in a semi-circle behind him. 'He has sent me with the stock. You give me the gold and the horses are yours.'

'Hang on, Pa,' Bull roared, inspecting the brands.

'These are our own dang-blasted nags. Look at the brands. Them used to be the Circle Dot.'

'Is something wrong, *señor*?' Enrique asked, mockingly. 'We bought these horses in good faith from a *gringo* only a week ago. He had a bill of sale from a ranch in Laredo.'

'You bet there's something wrong,' the Old Man shouted, going puce with frustrated anger under his tan. 'These broncs were stolen from us. We got to take them back.'

'No, we cannot allow you to do that, *señor*. I cannot return to Don Luis empty-handed. He would have me flogged.'

At that the three Durhams started hollering in unison, making wild threats, saying that they were taking the stock and that was that. But slowly they simmered down as they looked around at the half-circle of guns, the *vaqueros* sitting their horses, revolvers cocked, carbines at the ready.

'I don' wan' trouble, Señor Durham.' Enrique smiled, affably, at him. 'You give us gold. You take horses. It simple as that.'

'No way.' John Durham spotted a troop of *rurales* in their scarlet-lined capes and sombreros riding out from the town. He hailed them and began to explain his case in broken Spanish. 'These are our stolen stock. You come with us to the other side and see what the American Customs got to say.'

The *capitan* smiled suavely, consulted Enrique, and shrugged. 'There is nothing I can do. He has a bill of sale. The horses lawfully belong to Don Luis Arroyo.'

'Oh, yeah, you lousy greaser,' Bull shouted. 'You're in cahoots with him.' His hand had gone to the revolver in his belt. 'We ain't payin' a thousand dollars, no way.'

'I tell you what.' Enrique spread his hands, beaming benevolently. 'I let you have 'em for nine hundred gold.'

'Hold it,' the Old Man cried to Bull. 'Don't do nuthin' foolish. We ain't got a snowball's chance in hell. We been suckered, boys. But we need them broncs.'

He turned back to Enrique and pointed a finger in his face. 'You tell that Lance Silverlight I ever catch up with him he's a dead man. Eight hundred dollars. That's my top price.'

'*Que caballos tan hermosos!*' Enrique kissed his fingers. 'How can I let them go for so little. But to you, *amigo*, it's a deal.'

'Beautiful horses? Yeah, you bet they are.' Durham swung down, opened his and his sons' saddle-bags and paid out on the spot. 'They oughta be at this price, you bloodsuckers. I'm buying my own stock.'

He was about to leave when the *capitan* tugged his sleeve, and made a motion of thumb and fore-finger. '*Señor! Dinero!* One hundred dollar. You geev, pliz.'

'Give? You? What for?'

'For export licence. You no take *caballos* out of Mexico without licence. You come down. I write for you. It easy.'

'Yeah. It sure is, you sidewinder.' Durham clinked five golden eagles into his outstretched palm. 'OK? Right, let's go.'

'It pleasure do business with you,' Enrique called, spurring his mount and calling to his men to set the herd of mustangs moving. 'We help you take them over river. You see, we friend to the *Americanos*.'

'Pa,' Bull moaned as they rode off to the town, 'you get the feelin' these fellows are all laughin' at us?'

'Sure do,' John Durham grunted. 'It's the worst day's business I ever done. But there'll be a reckoning one day. You mark my words.'


Don Luis Arroyo had been summoned to meet the president's henchman, Ramon Corral, who had come from the capital, via Durango, to Monterrey, specially for this purpose.

When a man like Corral issued a summons, a man was not tardy. He was renowned for the way he had horrifically put down a rebellion by the Yaqui Indians, usurping their lands to become governor of that other northern state, Sonora.

His depravity was legendary and his estates ran into uncounted millions of acres, like those of the other leading *haciendados*, plundered from the *peons* and the Indians. By comparison with Ramon Corral, Don Luis was a small time rancher.

It was the don's turn to sweep off his sombrero and bow down on one knee as he was ushered into a study in the palace of the Nuevo Leon governor, who, after a few formalities and a glass of sherry, was summarily dismissed by Corral.

'*El presidente* received your epistle. He is pleased that you are vigilant on our northern border.' The moon-faced mestizo, Corral, lounged in a chair, his booted legs stuck out, his uniform hanging open to reveal a swarthy chest. 'We have information that the bandit Ignacio Parra is planning to meet a party of Texans who will sell him arms and ammunition. Our spies say that the meeting place will be at Camargo on the border, a hundred miles from your hacienda. We want you to take care of it.'

'Take care of it, *señor*?'

'Sure.' Corral lit a thick cigar. 'Your *vaqueros* must know the area like the back of their hands. The *rurales*, on the other hand, stand out like a sore thumb in their uniforms. They are a dumb bunch, the scum of the prisons, only good for killing. They have been chasing Parra futilely. They can get no information from the *peon* even if they flog them to the white of the bone. Your men, on the other hand, could go under cover, be unsuspected, arrange an ambush, wipe out this young wolf for once and for all.'

'This Parra, *señor*,' Don Luis faltered, 'I do not know a lot about him.'

'Why not? It is your duty to know,' Corral roared. 'Surely you know that he is an ignorant, untutored peasant? He killed a landowner and fled to the hills. He maybe young but he is bloodthirsty and ambitious. He has been building up contacts with revolutionaries.'

'*Si, senor*. I know this, but little else of him or his whereabouts.'

'It is your duty to know,' Corral growled, picking up a plaited rawhide bullwhip to send it snaking across the room and, with a crack, sever one of the governor's candlesticks. He grinned as Arroyo jumped. 'Find out all about him. Kill him. That is the order of the president. If you succeed we will get rid of that old fool who was here just now. The governorship of the state will be yours and all that goes with it. You understand.?'

'*Si*, I understand, *señor*. I will do my best.'

'Your best is not good enough.' Corral glowered at him, mockingly, coiling the whip. 'You must adopt *my* methods if you wish to succeed. Show no mercy.'

'Yes,' Don Luis said. 'I heard that you ran out of rope hanging Yaquis.'

Corral laughed, brutally. 'Yes, we had to keep cutting them down and using the same rope over again. We strung up so many on one branch the whole damn tree collapsed.'

'Is there anything else I should know, *señor*?'

'No. You make your own rules. But I wouldn't advise you to fail, Don Luis.' He shrugged and waved a dismissive hand. 'You can go.'

'*Gracias, señor*. I will do everything in my power to capture him.'

When he got back to his hacienda Don Luis had his prisoners brought before him. 'You are in luck my friends. You, in particular, *Americano*. That is, if you know how to use this gun we took from you.'

Don Luis was sitting at his banqueting table with his concubine, Teresa, beside him. 'I need men for my private army. Would you be willing to work for me? If so' – he pushed Silverlight's Lightning across the polished surface – 'show me what you can do.'

A flood of power made Lance smile as he grasped hold of his weapon. He was half-tempted to shoot the *haciendado* through the heart – that would show him – but a glance around at the armed *vaqueros* up on the balcony and around the room changed his mind. 'I can snuff a candle with this at thirty paces,' he said. 'Is that good enough?'

'Let's see if you can extinguish the candles of that chandelier at the far end of the room.'

'That's a tall order.' The Lightning was a heavy handgun – weighing two and half pounds, in fact – and a man needed a strong grip to hold it steady aimed. The chandelier was a good fifty paces away. He raised the revolver with his right hand, steadying his wrist with his left, aligned the pin-head of the front sight with the v-notch of the rear sight, and drawled, 'Anythang Hickok can do....'

Don Luis smiled and drew his own revolver, a magnificent weapon, its fifteen-inch barrel gold-engrained and studded with diamonds, a golden colt rampant on its ivory grip. 'You succeed I pay you one hundred dollars a week to work for me. You miss, I send you back to be hanged.'

There were five flickering candles in the chandelier hanging by the far door. *Pa-dang!* The huge hall reverberated to the explosion and the whine of the ricochet. A serving maid screamed and jumped for cover. 'Yeah, you better watch yourselves,' Lance warned, but the first candle was out.

He lowered the gun, regaining confidence, then brought it up fast. Two, three, four, five shots rang out and bullets rebounded like angry bees about the walls. 'Yeah.' Silverlight let out his held breath. 'Got every one.'

He blew down the hot barrel as acrid black powder smoke rolled about him, spun the revolver on his finger and pointed it at Don Luis. 'Do I pass?'

For seconds, the landowner's eyes locked with the Texan's, then he smiled. 'Bravo! Excellent shooting. A hundred dollars it is. Put that away. Come and join the meal. The steaks are getting cold.'

Pedro hesitated, not sure whether he was invited. 'You want to see my shooting, your excellency?'

'No, sit down, *peon*. I expect you're just average. I'll pay you twenty-five dollars a week, in pesos. We don't need any more shooting tonight. It's lucky nobody got killed.'

'Can I take a look at your piece?' Silverlight asked, extending his hand, and, after initial hesitation, Don Luis handed it across. 'Whoo! Some shooter. How much did this set you back?'

'A thousand dollars,' Don Luis announced, proudly. 'I had it specially made at the Frankford Arsenal, Pennsylvania. You know it?'

'Heard of it,' the Texan replied, pulling up his chair and getting stuck in to the steaks and tortillas. 'Wine, yeah, don't mind if I do.' He watched his glass being filled by a serving wench. 'Mine cost fifteen bucks at McNamara's store.' He slid the fancy shooter back across. He gave Teresa, who was bedecked in evening dress and diamonds, a conspiratorial wink and drawled, 'Seems to pay, don't it, gal, working for his excellency?'

The girl jagged back her lips in a grimace. 'It was not of my choosing.'

Don Luis laughed, touching her hand. 'This poor deluded young creature still has quaint ideas about liberty, equality and fraternity. Soon she will learn that might is right, the lash rules Mexico. Democracy might work in the States, but not here. Juarez proved that. All this nonsense she spouts about free elections! Pah! You Yankees think you're pretty smart. We lost the war to you and Santa Anna surrendered vast tracts of our lands. But under President Diaz the nation of Mexico will be strong again.' He suddenly sprang to his feet, raising his glass. 'To our great benefactor and death to all who oppose him.'

'*Salud*!' Lance Silverlight raised his goblet. What did he care? He was more interested in getting a refill of the heady sparkling stuff. 'Yeah, to *el presidente*. Do I take it I'll be working for him?'

'Of course, which means we can kill whoever we care to, especially if they are suspected rebels. There is a man called Ignacio Parra, a bandit who leads a gang of scum. They call themselves freedom fighters. We have information, elicited under torture, that tomorrow a bunch of Texans will meet them to sell a shipment of arms. We will ride to try to intercept them.'

'So, there's likely to be killing?'

'Naturally. We will wipe out these scum, the arms will be ours, and the president will be well pleased.'

'Doesn't such killing bother you?' the girl asked. 'These men are fighting for my country's freedom.'

Silverlight shrugged and lit one of Don Luis's

cigars, puffing out smoke. 'A war's a war. Your boyfriend here says they are bandits. I'll have to take his word for it. If the president's on our side that makes it legal, don't it? And I guess killing's what I'm being paid for.'

'You disgust me, all of you.'

Silverlight grinned at Don Luis. 'She feels purty strong about this, don't she?'

'Ach, she still holds a torch for that lawyer she was engaged to. He had the nerve to come here ordering me to let her go. I had him flogged and he crawled back to Monterrey on his knees. Perhaps I should have you kill him for me?'

'You sound like a merry bunch.' Lance got to his feet. 'Say, any chance of gittin' a shave an' a bath 'fore we go? These black clothes don't show the dirt much but they're beginning to whiff. They could do with laundering. And how about something on account, say fifty dollars?'

'No, nothing on account.' Don Luis raised his hand. 'I will pay you when you have earned it.' He signalled one of the serving girls. If very dark she was quite a chubby little thing, with eyes that glowed saucily .'Rosita here will tend you in the tub and wash your rags, and' – the *aristo* smiled in his vain manner – 'she used to be a favourite of mine. Any other service you require you have only to ask her.'

'Waal,' Lance drawled with a grin. 'It *has* been quite a while. And I reckon Marie Durham's lost to me. So' – he reached out for a bottle of wine – 'don't mind if I take this along?'

Don Luis waved his hand, expansively. 'Be my

guest. But be ready to ride at dawn, Mr Silverpurse.'

'– light,' Lance corrected him, putting an arm around Rosita's tubby waist and lurching somewhat squiffily away, followed by Pedro. 'Hey, *amigo*, you better find a gal of your own. We cain't both have her. Or can we?' He spun a silver dollar. 'Which do you fancy? Heads or tails?'

# EIGHT

'This looks like 'em coming.' Luther Sargent had a beady eye to a brass telescope as he sat his horse and surveyed the south bank of the Rio Grande. Out of a cloud of dust had appeared a motley band of *vaqueros* riding at a fast lope on their spirited horses. 'Keep your guns cocked, boys. If I got any doubts we kill 'em all.'

Luther was a man of a dangerous religion. He believed in the gun as the answer to any prayer. He was attired in old frontier style, wide skirts of chaps encasing his legs, a double-breasted canvas shirt, a wide, fringed bandanna loosely tied around his scrawny throat. The brim of his Stetson was bent back at the front, his white hair hanging to his shoulders, and long moustachios climbed below his chin. His sharp, hawklike features were weatherbeaten and lined with crow's feet. These were not wrinkles but battle lines!

'You sure that's them?' his partner, Harold Bluetit, queried, nervously. He was rigged out in city style, dusty suit and derby hat. It was he who had made contact in San Antonio with the little Mexican gent, Modesto, who was planning to invade his homeland. 'We don't want no mistakes.'

'Well, they ain't *rurales*, thass one thang,' Luther snarled. 'If they got the coin the guns are their'n.'

Behind them was the wagon containing the cargo in crates labelled, 'Plough shares' and 'Barbed wire' just in case any nosy customs officers might come along. But they had chosen their rendezvous a hundred miles up-river from Brownsville just below Falcon Lake, a lonesome spot even for these sparsely populated parts.

Luther raised a gauntleted hand and hollered across the wide river, '*Hola*! We're over here.'

The temperature was well over 100 degrees on Gabriel Fahrenheit's scale and how he managed to wear the hot, heavy *chaparreras* and gloves without sweating was a mystery. Some said he had ice in his veins, not blood.

Luther had begun his killing career in Montana in '63 working as a road agent for Sheriff Henry Plummer's band. In the mining community of Virginia City, a man was shot every day there, not always of necessity, sometimes merely for fun.

When he had been run out of Montana by the vigilantes, he had progressed southwards, looting, shooting, raping, scalp-hunting, robbing banks, railroads and stagecoaches. He had lost count of how many men, women and children he had killed, sometimes merely for sadistic pleasure, or to let them know who was boss.

In middle age he had become one of the most

feared of the flotsam of the frontier, now occupying his time mostly running guns and contraband across the border. The average age for a peaceable citizen was thirty-two in those parts. Most gunslingers rarely survived their mid-twenties (with notable exceptions like Earp and Cole Younger). So, to reach his mid-fifties was testament to Luther Sargent's ruthless cunning.

The Mexicans had come to a halt across the river, milling about looking for a good point to cross. 'They got some spare pack-horses with 'em so it must be them,' Luther drawled.

'I don't like it,' Harold Bluetit muttered. 'I got a funny feeling.' He, too, had done his share of killing, but preferred to shoot a man in the back, sometimes merely because they had laughed at his name. 'Be sure you ask them the password, Luther.'

'Aw, ye're an ole woman,' Luther muttered. He called to the thirty mixed bunch of 'breeds and white trash who rode with him, 'All right, boys, fan out behind the wagon. We wanna see these buzzards' cash 'fore we part with any guns.'

Led by Enrique, the band of *vaqueros* were swimming their mounts across. When they reached the shallows and splashed on to the northern shore, Luther loosened his leg-iron, his Smith & Wesson in its holster, and examined them. The riders, in greasy leathers and draped with *bandoleers* of bullets, in wide, decorated sombreros, might well be *bandidos*. Then, on the other hand, they might not.

They were accompanied by a grey-haired man of Luther's years, attired too expensively to be true, and riding a very feisty stallion, its harness and saddle flashing silver.

'Who's he?' he asked, his eyes narrowed.

'He is a friend of Señor Modesto.' Enrique grinned broken teeth at him. 'Did he not tell you about Don Luis? He supports our fight, brings us information from the city. He is the man with the money.'

'So, who are you?'

'I'm am called Ignacio Parra.' Enrique certainly looked swarthy and ugly enough to fit the bill. 'You have heard of me?'

'Yeah, I've heard of you. So what you got to say to us?'

'I am Parra, I fight for Meh-ico,' Enrique roared, doing a fine impersonation. 'I want to buy guns. What more you wan'?'

The *rurales* had caught one of Parra's men – betrayed by a jealous woman lover when he had called on her in the village of Agualegas – and when he had been hung by his heels over their fire he had finally revealed the location of the hand over of the arms and the passwords to be used.

'They make a good pig's head stew in Camargo,' Enrique grinned at Luther. 'You want to come across and eat with us, *gringo*?'

'Pig's head stew, eh?' Luther was still sitting his horse. He felt more at home in the saddle, rarely and reluctantly abandoning it to descend to the level of mere mortals. 'That's what Modesto told us, didn't he, Hal? The password?'

'That's right. But we want to have their gold 'fore

we go any further, Luther.'

'No,' Enrique replied. 'You don't see no gold 'til we see what you got for us.'

'Oh, *Madre de Dios!*' Don Luis spoke for the first time. 'We have got to show some trust. They wouldn't have come all this way for nothing.' He swung down from the stallion, spurs jingling, and unbuckled his saddle panniers. He removed several pouches of silver and gold, the dollars received for the stolen horses, and tossed them to Luther Sargent and Harold Bluetit. 'Real American dollars. A hundred in each pouch. You satisfied?'

'Yeah.' Luther examined each pouch, tested some of the coins with his teeth. 'Good ole US cartwheels, sure 'nough. Right, let's do business.'

He rode over to the wagon, pulled off the tarpaulin cover at the back and called, 'Git these crates out, boys.'

He jogged back to Enrique and Don Luis and glanced at a dark-haired youth with icy blue eyes, dressed in black leather. He was different to the other riders. 'Who's he?'

'I'm just a hired hand.' Lance smiled at the older man. 'But I support any rebel cause. That's why I'm here.'

'Yeah?' Luther never trusted any man with a flowery manner of speech. And this one looked like he might be able to handle himself. 'You know anything about guns?'

'Sure.'

'So, take a look at those. The best.'

Silverlight stepped down to join Don Luis and

examined the hardware as the cases were broken open. He picked out a Ballard rifle, and gave a whistle of awe. 'Very nice. You got ammunition for these?'

'Two crates of it,' Bluetit said. 'This is brand new stock, straight off the production line. Each of these rifles will readily sell for a hundred and fifty dollars. You can have 'em for a hundred each.'

'Mind if I try it?' Lance opened a box of slugs, inserted three into the magazine of the Ballard, levered one into the breech, raised the rifle to his shoulder and took a pot at a cactus plant fifty yards away, splattering it. 'Nice action,' he murmured.

'They got a range of seven hundred and fifty yards,' Bluetit pointed out, as the sound of the explosion barrelled away across the river. 'Dead accurate at two hundred and fifty yards. Of course, that ain't taking into account Mex shooting, which ain't that hot.'

'Yeah, the stupid bastards don't generally even take aim,' Luther jeered from horseback. 'Jest blam away from the hip at all an' everythang. These are too good for 'em. Top quality. There's some older Spencer carbines in them other crates. Ex-war department. How much we asking for them, Hal?'

'They can have 'em for forty dollars each.' Bluetit licked a pencil and did his sums in a scrappy notebook. He counted the sacks of gold. 'You're going to need more than this, gentlemen. Another five thousand three hundred dollars.'

'We can pay in silver pesos.' Don Luis had raided his own safe in readiness for the transaction. Rifles did not come cheap. 'Show him, Enrique.'

'Enrique?' Luther's hand tightened on the butt of his revolver as he eyed the Mexican *segundo*, suspiciously. 'I thought your name was Ignacio?'

Enrique shrugged his shoulders. 'I have many names. Enrique, Ignacio, Manolo. Next week I might be somebody else.' He busied himself getting the silver out of the saddle-bags and plonking it down on the wagon tailboard where Bluetit could count it. 'See, *señor*. Many pesos.'

'Well, it's silver, so I guess it'll do,' the arms dealer said. 'That's fine for the rifles and ammo.' He stashed the pouches of gold and silver away in the wagon. 'You want to see our prize possession?'

'What would that be?' Don Luis asked.

'You ever heard of a Gatling gun?' Bluetit ordered two of his helpers to haul a box out to the tail board. He lifted the lid and picked from its straw wrapping a shiny steel machine-gun with a bronze breech housing. 'If Custer had taken one of these beauties along like he was supposed to, he would never have got wiped out.'

''Hey, *bueno*!' Enrique shouted. 'Just what my troops need. How much you wan' for this?'

'A thousand dollars,' Bluetit said. 'No haggling.'

'You have the ammunition?' Don Luis asked.

'It's manufactured by Colt. Straightforward army issue for shoulder arms, .45-70 calibre. Here's the magazine.' He inserted the long box magazine upright into the top of the bronze mounting. 'Simplicity itself. Feeds in by gravity.'

'And how do you operate it?' Don Luis asked.

'You assemble it to this tripod, see? A couple of

bolts. There we are! You can raise it with that winding mechanism.' Bluetit was enthusiastic to demonstrate his knowledge. 'And you just keep turning that little handle to fire it. It's got a range of a thousand yards.'

'Really?' Don Luis glanced about him and winked craftily at Enrique. 'Yes, I will pay you another thousand for this.' Most of Luther's gunmen had dismounted and were on foot in a semi-circle behind the wagon, up on a rise of rocks overlooking them, their carbines in their hands in readiness. 'Ignacio, do you have that other cash?'

It was the agreed signal, and, hearing it, Lance backed his black horse away from Luther who looked like a dangerous *hombre*. Don Luis was kneeling down peering along the barrel of the Gatling. He took hold of the turning handle. 'Like this?'

'Hey, it's loaded,' Bluetit yelled. 'Don't touch that!' But, too late, he was the first one to be bowled over by a stuttering blast from the machine-gun as Don Luis then turned it upon the semi-circle of gun merchants, coolly turning the handle, mowing them down as they tried to fire at him. They didn't have a chance, collapsing like ninepins as Don Luis traversed the Gatling in an arc on its pedestal. 'How about that!' he cried, a madness in his eyes. '*Si, viva* Mexico.'

There was consternation as the gun-runners attempted to escape. Most of them were caught in a slow-motion balletic frieze, arms thrown upwards, as Don Luis raked them with the Gatling's spitting lead. He was laughing hysterically now, like a child with a new toy. He swivelled the machine-gun back and forth and some of the horses were caught in the crossfire, screaming, whinnying, crashing down as bullets ploughed into them.

Luther Sargent was whirling his mount, furiously, aiming his revolver at the Mexican *charros*, who were almost as surprised as him, blasting three to eternity. He was trying to control his plunging mount and get a bead on Don Luis, but, as he did so, Lance shot the revolver spinning out of his hand. Luther turned, his face contorted with anger and pain, stared at the blue-eyed Texan and screamed, 'I'll be back.'

Silverlight would have taken another shot at the wild frontiersman, but he was too busy trying to get out of the way of Don Luis's crazily spraying bullets. Luther jerked his mustang's head around and set off, followed by two of his men, racing along the bank of the river to disappear into some cottonwoods. A couple of *vaqueros* gave shrill cries and went haring after them.

Suddenly there was silence, except for the piteous groans of the injured. The Gatling's bullets were spent. Don Luis looked around, his hair hanging over his eyes, as if disappointed that his fun had ceased. 'Ai-ee! *Hombre!*' he called to Lance. 'How you theenk they like that? We turn tables on them, eh?'

'You can say that again,' Lance muttered. 'What you might call a massacre.'

'Ah, we say in Mexico, the bloodier the holier. This was revenge for the invasion of my country by you lousy *Americanos*.'

'Yep. Maybe.' Silverlight, still on horseback, his

Lightning warily at the ready in case there were any survivors, was taking a look at the fallen bodies. 'What we going to do with these wounded? There's one here with a shattered arm.'

'I will show you what we do.' Don Luis retrieved his sombrero, strode across to the one in question, a scruffily dressed cowboy little older than Lance. He drew his diamond-encrusted revolver and pointed it at his forehead. 'No, mister, please,' the young man begged. Don Luis cocked the hammer and fired, splattering his brains. 'His sufferings on this earth are over. Let God sort it out.'

Lance winced with distaste as the other *vaqueros* carried out 'mercy killings' even of one of their own injured men, quickly kneeling to go through their pockets, retrieve what valuables they could and, of course, their arms and ammunition.

'I see you don't have a liking for this sport.' Don Luis smiled up at him. 'You are too soft, *gringo*. It is the only way. *Para escarmiento de los criminales....* let this be a warning to other criminals.'

Enrique and the other *vaqueros* came riding back along the bank of the river. 'They got away,' he said.

'A pity. I do not like to leave witnesses. The *Americanos* can get touchy about us invading their territory although they don't mind invading ours. Still, if there is an inquiry we can blame it on Ignacio Parra.'

Lance Silverlight looked around, somewhat at a loss, at all the bodies in their contorted death poses, the flies already zooming in at the blood, a line of ants busily attending in one's eyes, vultures circling up in the sky. 'Poor devils,' he said. But when a wounded man moved and groaned he spun around and shot him through the chest. 'Yeah, I guess it's the best way.'

'They were the scum of the frontier. They knew what to expect.' Don Luis slapped him on the shoulder. 'You are young. You have not yet grown used to killing.'

'No, but I'm learnin' fast. You're a good tutor.'

'Come on, we have a lot to do. We must get these weapons across the river. Enrique tells me you saved my life, you shot the revolver out of that *hombre's* hand when he was aiming at me. Here!' He thrust a pouch of silver dollars into Silverlight's hand. 'There is your first payment. You will see I am not ungrateful.'

'Waal,' Lance drawled. 'I guess you saved yourself a good few thousand dollars by not paying these rascals what they asked.'

'I certainly did.' Don Luis tapped his temple with a forefinger. 'You have to have it up here to succeed in life. I have got myself a fine new Gatling gun. I may well be made governor of Nuevo Leon. *El Presidente* is going to be well pleased.'

'Yeah, good work,' Lance muttered, hauling himself back on to Beater. 'How you gonna get this wagon across?'

'We will unharness the horses and float it across on ropes,' Enrique replied. He grinned tobacco-stained teeth. 'We have had a good day, eh, *gringo?*'

Silverlight smiled in his scoffing way and weighed the pouch of silver in his palm. 'Sure, you could say so.'

## STOLEN HORSES

\*

Don Luis Arroyo rode into Camargo on his proud stallion at the head of his band of bloodstained *vaqueros* and the wagon they had captured. It was a town like many others in Mexico, shady colonnades around a pot-holed plaza, folk in ragged whites and sombreros, with their carts and donkeys, going about their business. But because it was a border town it also flaunted many cantinas, bars and 'sporting houses'. The don and his men halted in front of one of these, romantically named, 'The Daughters of Eve'.

'It is time to celebrate, my friend,' he said. 'This is where they cook the famous pig's head stew.'

'I'll warn my stomach what to expect,' Silverlight replied, as he hitched his horse to the rail outside. 'How about the booze? No chance of any whiskey, I s'pose?'

'Ah, you must try the *aguardiente*. They brew it themselves.'

The brew, as its name implied, was firewater. Served in an earthenware mug, the first sup nearly blew Lance's head off. But the after effects spun his senses, hit him with a fireworks glow. Soon he had to hang on to the bar to stay upright amid the gang of garrulous, sweat-stained *vaqueros*. 'Let's sit this one out,' he said to Pedro.

They found a corner table and Pedro leaned his carbine against the wall. 'Hey, *hombre*, did you see all that gold and silver Don Luis got back?'

'I could hardly help not doing so.' Lance lit a

cheroot to steady his spinning head. 'Presumably you're thinking the same thing as me. How do we extricate it from his clutches?'

'You say you come to Mexico to get rich. Maybe the Lord has offered you this chance.'

'Surely we can work out some way of getting it and getting out?'

'I'll think about it over these *frijoles*.' They came with fatty chunks of the fabled pig's head, a pair of eyes floating on top. 'Christ! he gasped, as the red hot chilli peppers burned his mouth and he grabbed for his drink. 'The food is worse than the booze.'

'Do you mind if I have the pig's eyes?' Pedro scooped them out of the gravy and crunched them. 'They are the best part.'

Lance ate as much as he could and pushed his plate away. 'If you ask me chillis and beans and *aguardiente* has killed more Mexicans than all the bullets of your revolutions.'

'Ah, you Yanquees don't know how to live. Taste these wonderful *tortillas*. Do you get them in Texas?'

'No, thank God. And I think I'll pass on the Daughters of Eve if they are a specimen of them over there.'

A colossus in a corset and very little else, apart from some clinging *frou frou* of a ragged gown was sprawled on a horsehair sofa nearby, fanning her dark self as sweat runnelled into the creases of her many chins and sagging breasts. She gave Silverlight a cherubic smile.

'He's a hard swine, that Don Luis. We're gonna have to wait our chance, somehow, when his back's turned, steal his loot and head for the border, fast. I'm gonna have that gal of his, Teresa, too, before I go. We'll make for El Paso, get outa Texas, set ourselves up in New Mexico or Arizona. We'll be able to buy our own ranch.'

'Sounds good, *amigo*.' Pedro had his one eye on the fat one's companion, a skinny, parrot-nosed harlot sitting demurely alongside. Purple powder and garish rouge, liberally applied, failed to disguise her pocked complexion. 'But risky.'

'At least in Texas there's some kinda honour among thieves. Luther Sargent had gone to a lot of trouble to set up that deal. He expected to be paid in gold not lead.'

'A wolf like that should have been more wary.'

'Yeah, it was a damn fool thing to do, hand over a loaded Gatling gun to Don Luis. I could hardly believe it.'

'Luther is not a man I would care to bump in to again.'

'Nor me, neither.'

'If you're not interested in these charming ladies, I am.' Pedro got to his feet and smiled across at the parrot nose in her floral frock and little hat.

'Me, I'd rather have a bottle in my hand. I'll just sit here and try to figure out how to part that silver and gold from Don Luis.'

As if he had read his lips, Don Luis strode across from the carousing men. He was flushed by the success of his day's work. 'Ah, *caballeros*,' he greeted them. 'What plot are you hatching?'

Silverlight grinned at him. 'You'd be surprised.'

'Why, what do you mean?'

'Only joking, ole sport. We was just sayin' we'd like to stay in your employ a bit longer. It's kinda fun.'

'Good, you have made a wise decision, *gringo*. I value what you did for me today. You stick with me you will not regret it.'

'Yeah.' Lance nodded, thoughtfully. 'Maybe I won't.'

'Come, we must ride on through the night. We have a valuable cargo. These are dangerous parts to linger in for long. We must get back to the hacienda.'

'Too bad, Pedro, old pal,' Lance called across to the Mexican who had his arms around the beanpole whore. 'We gotta go.'

Pedro pushed the woman towards the back room and raised his fingers. 'Give me three minutes.'

# NINE

'Hey, git off.' Quince awoke with a start, kicking out at a growling, snarling beast that was gnawing at his foot. 'Git away from me.'

His left boot was half pulled off and, by the light of the camp-fire, he saw the green, glimmering eyes, the long snout and fangs of a coyote trying to pull the boot free. 'Hi-yagh!' he cried, awake now, and hurling a lump of rock at this scavenger of the plains, which was being watched by his pack of nervous fellow coyotes. Reluctantly they scattered, the boot-stealer, too, backing off as Quince reached for a smouldering brand from his fire and slung it at them.

'Dang me.' Quince tossed another log and watched the coyotes disappear into the night. 'Never thought a cowardly coyote would try to pinch my boots. They must be hungry.' He tried to revive his fire and looked across at Feathers. 'Everyone seems to be starving in this goddamned country.'

There was a glimmer of dawn in the sky. It was cold on this mountain plateau. He pulled his torn sheepskin jacket closer around him and warmed his hands at his small blaze. Best to be moving on. Though where he was going he had little idea. 'Whoo! For moments I thought I was dreaming there. Life wouldn't have been much fun with only one boot.'

It had been easy enough following the trail of the sixty stolen horses along the soft ground of the Neuces River, and not so difficult when they had branched off and headed south. But after he had swum his horse across the Rio Grande the trail had gone cold as he climbed across the hard rocky ground. They could be anywhere in the vast emptiness of northern Mexico. The only thing to do was just press on and ask around at the few and far-between villages he came to. The envious glances the *peons* gave his pony made him think they'd like to devour it. He was beginning to think he was lucky he hadn't had his throat cut in his sleep.

Quince breakfasted on coffee, and flapjacks baked in the ashes, gave Feathers – named for the feathers of hair around his hoofs – a handful of split corn and saddled-up. Best to put some miles behind him while the day was cool. How long he would go on searching for Lance Silverlight he was not sure. Maybe give it six more days, or so. He had no wish to spend all of his thirty dollars and be destitute in an unknown country. The high hopes with which he started out were beginning to fade. He wondered if he would be a match for Lance Silverlight and Pedro even if he caught up with them. The more he thought about it the more it seemed like an impossible mission. And the memory of Marie, his hopeless passion for her, made him even more despondent. 'What the hell am I doing here?' he asked himself. 'I ain't a damn bounty hunter.'

Suddenly a bullet spurted into the dust making his pony whinny and snort his alarm. There was the crack of a rifle report and another as a slug whined past his head to ricochet off the rocks. 'Hey, greengo!' a voice called shrilly and, looking up, Quince saw standing on the top of a pile of rocks a thin-faced Mexican with a wispy beard, an ancient rifle smoking in his hands. 'What you doin' in my land?'

There was a cackle of laughter as about twenty other, similarly ragged, men revealed themselves. Draped with belts of bullets, in ponchos and battered sombreros, guns in their hands, they seemed to be mightily amused by the young Texan's surprise.

Quince's heart dropped into his boots. Hot damn, he thought. There could be little doubt about it. He had walked right into a nest of bandits. The only thing to do was to try to brave it out. 'Howdy,' he called. 'Nice to meetcha. I ain't seen a soul for days.'

This only set them off laughing some more as the tall, razor-faced one bounded down and poked at him with his rifle. 'Welcome. My name is Ignacio Parra,' he announced in Spanish. 'Would you kindly surrender your wallet. Be assured it is for a good cause.'

Quince had been brought up on the border and had naturally picked up the tongue. So he replied in frontier Spanish, 'I have very little, *señor*. A few dollars which I need, myself. I have no argument with you. My argument is with a man called Lance

Silverlight, perhaps you have seen him. He's about my age. Wears a black leather coat, dark glasses. You can't mistake him.'

Parra shrugged. 'No, I have not seen him. Just hand over your wallet, boy. And that carbine, and we may let you keep your life.'

Another bandit had arrived and was looking at Feathers' teeth, obviously planning on depriving Quince of his pony, too. A villainous, broken-toothed character, he had a razor-sharp machete in his hand. 'Shall I keel him, Ignacio?' he growled.

'Maybe.' Parra snapped his fingers at Quince. 'Maybe not.'

Quince took five dollars in silver from his pocket. 'That's everythang I got,' he lied, hoping, somewhat without hope, that they wouldn't find the 25 in greenbacks in his boot. 'I'm just a wanderin' cowboy. You guys don't want to bother with me.'

'Don't we?' Parra looked disdainfully at the five dollars and tested one with his teeth. 'We shall see.' He strode away behind the rocks while the other with the machete kept a close eye on Quince. The bandit chief suddenly reappeared on horseback, followed by his men, mounted, too. 'Bring him with us,' he shouted, and set off in the opposite direction to which Quince had been going.

The man with the machete snatched Quince's carbine from the saddle boot. 'Follow them,' he shouted. 'And don't try anything. I will be behind you. It will give me pleasure to slice off your ears.'

Aristide Rojas, the lawyer, still bore the marks of the

beating he had received from Don Luis Arroyo's thugs when he rode out to the hacienda to protest about him holding Teresa Teran captive. Since then he had received death threats and his dog had been poisoned. It was only because he came from a prominent Monterrey family, he felt, that he was still alive. Rojas wanted to uphold the law, but he had reluctantly decided that the only way to remove the evil regime of Diaz was through armed struggle. To that end he had been in touch with the exiled politician, Modesto, in San Antonio, Texas, acting as a go-between and passing messages to freedom fighters like Ignacio Parra. But their latest plan to import arms for an insurrection had gone badly wrong.

Rojas had a handsome, wavy-haired Gallic air, the result of a liaison between his mother and a French officer when, some years before, that nation had briefly ruled Mexico.

It was a Saturday morning when Rojas held a free surgery for the poor of the town. A bunch of *peons* had filed in before him to complain that Don Luis Arroyo had usurped their land. Ragged hats in hands, they were gathered humbly before him. 'You say you signed this document and were told by Don Luis that it would guarantee you possession of the common lands granted to you by Benito Juarez. It says nothing of the sort.'

'We know that now, *señor*. But we cannot read,' their spokesman said. 'Don Luis tricked us.'

'It's terrible,' Rojas muttered. 'You have signed away all your land to him. What can I do? Charge him in the courts as a swindler? What hope would we have?'

'What can *we* do, *señor*? Our families are starving.'

'Diaz controls the Press. Any editor who speaks the truth is thrown into jail. He controls the legislature. If I took this to court they would laugh at me.' He handed the document back. 'I am sorry, my friends. There remains only one thing left to us.'

'What, *señor*?'

'To fight.' Rojas took his revolver from his drawer, stuffed it in his suit pocket. 'You have convinced me. What we need is action. If you will excuse me.' He strode to the door. 'I must go. The time has come for extreme measures.'

He hurriedly went to his house, changed his clothes, saddled his horse, leapt into the saddle, and went galloping out of Monterrey, his coat tails flying, whipping the beast from side to side, throwing caution to the winds.

It was a parched land Aristide Rojas rode across. A land of brown dust, red rocks, cactus, sage and mesquite. A land of thorns. To him the twisted shapes of the tortured yucca seemed to represent the people's suffering. Not that a revolution would alter the landscape, but if wells were sunk deep at strategic points in this barren northern plateau he believed it could be made to flourish. But who in the Mexican hierarchy had anytime for such crazy ideas? Officialdom, from the lower to the higher, was intent, it seemed, only in greasing its collective palms. The bribe – *el mordida* – was endemic in

Mexico. The future could go to the devil.

The young lawyer had cast aside his city suit and had dressed in a light shirt, buckskin jacket, riding breeches, boots, and a Panama hat to make the long journey to Hidalgo. Reports had appeared in both the American and Mexican journals of a massacre of Americans, admittedly illegal arms dealers, on the north bank of the Rio Grande opposite Camargo. The blame was being laid at the feet of the National Liberation Party, in particular the 'rebel leader' Ignacio Parra. A lot of hot air was being spouted about invasion of the States' territorial border. It had not done their cause any good at all. The party was being painted as a band of murderous, robbing brigands.

What had happened? Had Parra betrayed their trust? Was he really just a bandit at heart?

It was not the only question that tormented Aristide. His whole life was a tangle of woe.

He was haunted constantly by the fate of the beautiful Teresa Teran, half-crazed by thoughts of the humiliations she was having to bear. He had tried to take her case to the courts but had been shown a phoney letter by the governor purporting to say she had gone to live with Don Luis of her own free will. He had been warned to forget her.

Rojas rode for much of the day towards some distant hills, purple in their heat-haze. There had been barely a spot of rain since December and it was only the altitude and slight breeze made the heat bearable.

The adobe shacks of Hidalgo had come into sight

and Aristide walked his horse down the unpaved, rutted main street. Everywhere there was the customary evidence of dirt, disease, ignorance and superstition: half-naked children crawling in the dust with grubbing pigs; starving curs running up to yap at his horse's heels. A typical *casa* had a small patch of maize and cotton, a few scraggy hens, a turkey perched on the roof, an *olla* of water and a string of red chillies hanging outside from a rafter beam, a young woman coming to the door, wrapped in her *rebozo*, to stare at him as he passed. Past, present and future children: a toddler clinging to her legs, flies sucking at his inflamed eyes, a baby at her breast, and the next in her swollen belly. How many would survive?

Outside a *cantina*, a row of men were sitting leaning against a wall, dozing beneath their sombreros. As Rojas dismounted, letting his horse drink at the village tank, a hideously deformed beggar wheedled alms. He pressed some coins into the man's hand and entered the shady ... well, it could hardly be called a restaurant, more a food-sty. And, as always, the flies were present at the feast.

On a griddle were fried maguey worms and grasshoppers. Rojas declined the offer of a fatty slice of fried pig-skin and ordered a beer. It was lukewarm and tasted like rusty water.

The *cantina* did not run to chairs, only mats on the floor. On one was a thin man with unkempt beard and hair, wiry and weatherbeaten, in a grimy shirt, cowhide pants, and knee-boots He had a gunbelt slung diagonally and a revolver shoulder-hung. His high cheekbones and narrow eyes gave him the look of a latter day Genghis Khan. The Chinese had settled on Mexico's coastline and one must have mated with Ignacio Parra's Indian mother.

'So what happened?' Rojas asked, as he sat beside him and leaned his back against the wall. 'You've been getting a bad press.'

'It is all lies.' Parra stared ahead, arrogantly. 'We were betrayed. Someone informed on us. The *rurales* were waiting for us as we approached Falcon Lake. We were forced to turn tail. We had a running battle for twenty miles and were lucky to escape. Meanwhile someone else had met the *Americano* arms dealers. He and his men killed them and stole what should have been ours.'

'Any idea who it was?'

'Don Luis Arroyo. I have since discovered he was seen with his men and a closely guarded wagon in Camargo that day.'

'I guessed as much. What now?'

'How should I know?' Parra tossed his hands. 'He is too strong for us to attack and now he has the machine-gun we were hoping for.'

'You still have the gold and silver we raised to pay for the arms?'

'It is safe. I am not a thief like Arroyo. I only rob those who deserve to be robbed. I fight against Porfirio Diaz and for the future of Mexico.'

A portrait of Diaz, much be-medalled, heavily moustached, strict, but smiling benevolently, had been copied and issued on posters to nearly every small town, those accessible, that was, through the mountain passes of Mexico.

'Look at the great father,' Parra jeered, making a couple of *peons* stare at him with alarm. 'The fat pig. A bullet is too good for him. I would tear that poster down but it would only bring punishment on the village.'

A gap-toothed *hombre* named Manolo, sitting next to him, swished his machete. 'When I get to him they will have a jigsaw puzzle at the resurrection. That goes for Don Luis, too. I will cut them to tiny pieces.'

For the first time Rojas noticed a youth in a greasy Stetson, torn shirt and jeans, obviously an American, sitting glumly alongside them. 'Who's he?'

'I dunno. We found him wandering through the mountains. I thought it unwise for any more *Americanos* to be found dead so I brought him along. Maybe we can use him as a hostage?'

'These men are holding me against my will,' Quince protested, 'after robbing me. If you're a lawyer can't you do something about it?'

'I will see no harm comes to you. What are you doing in Mexico?'

'He says he is chasing an *Americano* horse-thief called Silverlight, a gunslinger who rigs himself out in black leather. My spies tell me that this man is riding with Don Luis.'

'He is?' Quince exclaimed. 'But Don Luis is a friend of my boss, John Durham.'

'You don't know Don Luis. He is a friend of no man.'

'Where can I find him?' Quince asked.

Rojas and Parra exchanged glances. 'Not far from

here,' Rojas said. 'But to go there would be suicidal. I know, I have tried, and am lucky to be still alive.'

'Maybe it's the only way?'

'It is an impregnable fortress,' Rojas warned. 'He has forty armed men.'

'No, the boy speaks true.' Manolo jumped to his feet and brandished his machete. 'We must attack. We have taken too much.'

'*Si*,' Parra growled, 'better to die in the saddle than live on our knees under the lash of Diaz. Come! We must go.'

'Looks like I'm out-voted,' Rojas said, with a shrug, getting up, too. 'So, I am ready. What have I to lose?'

'Hang on,' Quince interjected. 'If I fight with you I want to take Lance Silverlight alive. I gotta take him back.'

'Sure, why not?' Parra said. 'What do we want with him?'

'And, before we go.' Quince caught hold of Parra's sleeve. 'How about my carbine back? An' my five dollars?'

'Ha!' The bandit leader hooked a bony, muscular arm around the wrangler's neck. ' You know, you are a good kid, for a *gringo*.' He banged his own chest with his fist. 'You got heart.'

# TEN

The sun was beginning to fall as Lance Silverlight came from the room he and Pedro had been allotted in the former monastery. He strolled along the balcony past Don Luis's master bedroom. The door was ajar and he glimpsed Teresa inside sitting before her dressing-table. He glanced down to the banqueting hall where Don Luis was sitting at the head of the table taking dinner with most of his *vaqueros*, those who were not on guard outside or still out on the range. Lance winked at Pedro and pushed silently inside the bedroom.

'What do you want?' the girl asked, listlessly. Hearing the jingle of spurs as Lance trod across the room she obviously thought it was Don Luis returned.

'You!' Lance wound his hand around her mouth and dragged her off her dressing stool, propelling her backwards to throw her across the bed. He rolled on top of her and groped for her breasts as she wriggled and protested, kicking out. 'Pedro,' he hissed.

'Tear up that sheet. We'll tie this hellcat for our later entertainment.'

Teresa struggled as she was bound hand and foot to the bed and tightly gagged. 'Don't worry,' Lance said, with his white-toothed smile. 'We're going to save you.'

The *haciendado* had set up the Gatling gun on its tripod on his balcony outside the open window, from where it gave him a commanding position to rake, if necessary, the wide stretch of courtyard across to the main gate in the high walls. It would, he believed, make him even more impregnable. Lance hoisted the contraption and at Pedro's signal, carried it out through the door. The one-eyed Mexican had walked along to the guard on their side of the balcony, asked for a light, and, as it was being offered, eased a knife through the man's ribs. He had succumbed with hardly a sound.

Meanwhile, Don Luis was down below getting stuck into suckling pig and goblets of wine, boasting about his part in the Battle of Monterrey in 1846 when he had personally bayoneted three US Marines, or so he said, and the retreat to Bueno Vista. 'It is true we were defeated by the American armies but we could have won if we were better led.' He had told the tale many times before but none of his men was inclined to tell him so. They were happy enough gobbling down their roasted pork and vino.

'Look at the pigs,' Lance muttered, as he balanced the machine-gun on a table top and poked its snout over the balcony. 'They are in for a surprise. Cover me, *amigo*.'

There were two other guards as yet unaware of them on the far side of the balcony, which ran all around the high-walled banqueting hall. 'Take them out,' he said, 'when I start shooting.'

Lance gripped the butt of the Gatling into his shoulder, checked the ammunition chamber was fixed tight, and gave an initial turn to the trigger handle. A rat-a-tat of half-a-dozen bullets sent Arroyo's half-eaten suckling pig flying, splattering him and Enrique with gravy. 'Testing,' Silverlight said and grinned down at the *haciendado*. 'Hey, Don Luis, howja like a taste of your own medicine?'

The whole company froze, one with a leg of greasy turkey to his half-open mouth, another belching over an *olla* of wine in his fist. There was a look of momentary surprise on each face, which turned to apprehension, and sudden activity as they scrambled to pull out their arms, then fear and pain as a line of bullets stuttered out, cutting through them. Those on the far side of the long table threw up their arms, jerking in spasms as the stream of bullets tumbled them from their chairs to fall back in agonized contortions.

Lance giggled maniacally, his black hair tumbled over his eyes, and cried, 'How about that?'

'No!' Don Luis shouted out with horror as he sat in his big oak chair, seemingly transfixed, and stared up at the American who had turned the tables on him, stared into the deathly hole of the barrel of his own machine-gun. 'No! Pliz! I pay you anything.'

'You sure will, buddy,' Lance gritted out, and swung the Gatling back on its tripod to start at the end of the near side row of *vaqueros*, laughing hysterically, as they tried to jump and duck to escape, methodically running along the line, blasting them into eternity, or whatever lay beyond the other side of life.

Pedro had been waiting for the two guards opposite to come to their senses and take aim at the machine-gunner. He liked to give a man a chance. It heightened the excitement. But, as they jerked up their carbines, he coolly took out each man. One screamed and toppled back against the wall, streaking it with blood as he slid down. The other, hit in the abdomen by the .45 calibre slug, doubled-up and toppled over the balcony to hit the stone floor and lie still. 'There ain't nuthin' wrong with this ole cap'n' ball,' Pedro yelled, blowing down the smoking barrel. 'Go on, hit 'em, *amigo*.'

Silverlight had left Don Luis to last, gritting his teeth in a deadly smile, enjoying the sensation of power as he caused bloody havoc down below. 'Now for you, my friend.'

Enrique was on his feet, his heavy revolver in his hand, snarling as he loosed bullet after bullet up at the balcony. 'Unh!' He collapsed as Pedro's lead cut a hole through his heart, trying to speak for a few seconds as he grovelled around on the floor.

'*Si*, I repay you with interest, pig,' Pedro cried. 'You should learn to shoot. The gun-runner was right. You fire too wild.'

Don Luis had pulled his fancy diamond-encrusted revolver, but the fifteen-inch barrel did him little favours, or his jangled nerves come to that, as he sent every bullet every which way but the right one. Then he lost his cool and ran for the door.

Silverlight smiled as he squinted along the sights and traced his path, almost like a cat playing with a mouse. Don Luis tried frantically to open the door, locked at his own command to keep out assassins, turned and opened his arms, begging and praying. 'No, please, God, no!'

Lance turned the little handle and cut him to ribbons with a stream of lead. 'So long,' he said. He and Pedro looked around them, but, apart from the groans of expiring men, all was silent after the excitement. 'Hey, man,' Lance exclaimed, 'we did it. We're rich, *amigo*.'

But, suddenly, there were shouts from outside, a hammering on the door, which was unlocked and burst open, several men tumbling in. 'What's going on … your excellency?' one said, staring around, dazedly, at the dead men.

'Guess.' Lance and Pedro started shooting until there was not one left alive to bear witness.

'Well,' Lance said, after a while, and they had both calmed down. 'I guess that's that.'

He ran lightly down the curving staircase, looked down at Don Luis, and took the magnificent revolver from his grasp. 'One minute you got everythang, the next minute you got nuthin'. Ain't life a bitch?'

He picked up the remains of a bottle of wine by the neck and tipped its contents down his throat. The Adam's apple in his strong, bronzed throat jerked as he drank. 'That's better,' he said, and grabbed a roast duck, chewing at the breast. 'Gives you an appetite this sort of thing. Which reminds me.' He glanced up towards the bedroom. 'Teresa.'

'First things first, Lance,' Pedro was going through Don Luis's pockets and produced a bunch of keys. 'He got a big safe in his bedroom. That more important than some damn girl.'

'Yeah, you got your priorities right, old friend. Come on. Then we gotta get outa here.'

'What about any other *vaqueros*? If they heard the shooting they'll come in off the range.'

'Ach, I can deal with them.' Lance swallowed some more wine to wash down the duck. He pointed the expensive revolver at three or four cowering serving girls. 'You go out to the kitchens and the yard, tell them the big chief is dead. Tell everybody we don't aim to hurt them. In fact, why not celebrate? Open a few more casks of wine.'

As the women hurried off, Silverlight and Pedro ran up the stairs to the balcony and strode into the master bedroom. 'Gimme that key,' Lance said, and fiddled with the bunch impatiently, until he found one that fitted the safe. He swung open the door. 'Waal, look at that. Great Jehosophat! This guy really *was* rich.'

'It's all ours now, buddy.' Pedro scrambled to pull out pouches of gold and silver, stacks of currency, golden crucifixes looted from churches, ornaments and diamond necklaces, bracelets, cups inlaid with precious stones. 'Just look at this.'

'Hold on,' Lance said. 'Don't go gold crazy. Go see iffen you can find four strong gunny sacks and a coupla mules. We'll load up as much as we can carry.'

He turned to the girl on the bed, who was struggling anew against her bonds, gasping and chewing at her gag, her dark eyes staring at him with a mixture of fury and fear. 'Yeah, don' worry, Teresa. Just as soon as we're ready I'm gonna give you somethang to remember me by. I ain't Don Luis. You'll be cryin' out for more, gal.'

It was almost dark, the sun's last rays flickering away across the plain, as the gang of *bandidos* galloped towards the hacienda. 'Listen,' Quince shouted, as they hauled in before the outer wall's main gate. 'That shootin' sounded like it come from inside.'

'Sounded like our machine-gun,' the lawyer said. 'Perhaps Don Luis is practising.'

Manolo was taking a stick of dynamite from his bag to light and blow the main gate from its hinges, but Parra cautioned him. 'Wait! There seem to be no guards around. If we step softly we may catch this wolf in his lair.' He whirled his lariat, and sent it spinning to land over the gate's stout turret. 'Try not to make a sound, boys.'

The bandit chief climbed on to his saddle and swung out on the rope, hauling himself to the top of the gate. 'All clear,' he hissed down. 'Sounds like they're havin' a party. I'll open the gates.'

When he admitted the others, they rode through, carefully, guns in hands, fully cocked and loaded. The big door of the former monastery was open and some *peons* were in the act of pushing a huge cask of wine inside. Outside was a row of bloody bodies of *vaqueros*. Floating to the newcomers came jubilant cries of celebration. 'What the hell's going on?' Rojas asked.

'We'll soon find out,' Parra replied.

There was a light up in Don Luis's main bedroom, and suddenly from it came the scream of a girl, shrill above the other sounds. The lawyer tensed. 'That's Teresa,' he said 'I'm sure of it. Can you get a rope up to that balcony?'

'Sure.' Parra sent his lariat spinning again. 'We will give you three minutes then we go in the front.'

Rojas did not hesitate. He stuffed his revolver into his belt and began to clamber up the wall to the balcony. Quince lassoed another buttress on the balcony and followed him, hauling himself up hand over hand, making purchase against the adobe wall with his boot toes. They arrived at the top almost simultaneously and swung over on to the balcony.

Teresa screamed again as she tried to fight off Lance Silverlight, who had her pinned beneath him on the bed. 'I'll teach you, you bitch.' He cracked her across the face with his palm. 'Bite me, wouldja?'

Quince caught hold of Rojas as he drew his revolver and was about to charge through the open window. 'Don't kill him,' he croaked out. 'He's mine.'

One Eye Pedro Ocampo was busy with more important matters, carefully counting Don Luis's cash and stuffing it into sacks. He looked up as the curtain rustled and, fast as a rattler, went for his gun. But he wasn't fast enough. A startled look came over his face as the lawyer's first bullet ploughed into his shoulder, knocking him backwards. It turned to agony as the second hit him full in the chest. His false eye popped out and rolled across the floor as blood began to seep through his shirt.

'No-uh,' he stuttered out. 'Oh, *Madre de Dios.* I was rich.' He tried to claw at the gold coins and fell back lifeless.

Lance turned, surprised to see Quince, then made a grab for his Lightning, slung in its gunbelt from the bedpost. But Quince caught him by the shoulder, and with all the power of righteous fury, tensed his muscles and slammed his fist into his jaw.

Silverlight rolled from the bed. He had always been the better fighter when he was a kid, a wild one who other boys feared, and he kicked out at Quince, booting him in the abdomen. Then he made a grab for the dressing-table stool, smashing it over his shoulders.

'Uhh!' Quince was momentarily stunned, but he saw Lance kicking his left foot to try to get him again and just before it reached his head he caught the boot and twisted Lance off his feet. 'You devil's spawn,' he said.

Silverlight grinned in his mocking way as he took an ornamental lance from the wall and gripped it to thrust into the wrangler's body. 'How about this?'

Quince could have gone for his Colt but he didn't. He backed away and, as Lance lunged at him, he dodged aside and caught hold of it pulling his former friend towards him, tripping him and sending him flying. 'How about that?'

As Lance slithered across the polished floor, Quince leapt upon him and flailed blows to his jaw and head.

'OK.' Silverlight moaned, shrilly, blood trickling from his mouth and nose. 'You win. Don't ruin my looks.'

'Huh.' Quince paused over him, fist raised. 'They ain't gonna do you much good in future. You'll be dangling at the end of a rope.' He gave him one last punch for luck and Lance went out cold. Quince sat upon him, breathing hard. 'He ain't as tough as he thought he was.'

When he looked around, however, the lawyer, Rojas, was paying him little attention, sitting up on the bed, tenderly caressing and soothing Teresa. 'You are safe now,' he was murmuring. 'We will leave this accursed country and go to San Antonio. We will carry on the fight there with Modesto.'

Teresa clung to his shoulders and began to sob uncontrollably. 'How can you want me now?'

'What has happened to you is no fault of yours. One day you will forget,' Rojas said. 'I love you and you love me, that's what counts.'

'Oh, Aristide,' the girl gasped. 'I can't believe this. I had nearly given up all hope.'

'Never give up hope.' Quince grinned at them. 'Every cloud's got a silver lining. Well, I'll leave you two lovebirds and go see what's going on.'

Down in the banqueting hall was an amazing scene of celebration, as Ignacio Parra had discovered when he burst in. *Peons*, men, women, children, had crowded in and were greedily helping themselves to rich food and wine, the like of which they had never tasted. Even the *haciendado*'s few remaining *vaqueros* had surrendered their arms and were staggering about getting as drunk as lords.

Don Luis himself, or his corpse, had been placed in his banqueting chair at the head of the table, roped into place, and every time one of the Mexicans took a break from dancing around they would lean over and peer into his sightless eyes, proffer an insult, clout him about the head and go back to the dance.

One man was playing Pan's pipes, another banging a drum, while another *peon* had ridden his spavined horse into the chamber and was whirling it around among the reeling peasants. 'Soon the *rurales* will come,' he cried, waving a bottle. 'But until then we fiesta. For a day or two we are free.'

'One day, when we are ready,' Parra shouted, as he and his men helped themselves to wine from the great cask, 'we will be free for good. Viva Meh-hico!'

Quince grinned as he descended the staircase and saluted Parra. 'Well, it looks my runnin' into you boys was a stroke of luck for me,' he said. 'And you. You should go take a look at all Don Luis's assets.'

''Everything we take must go towards the cause,' Parra cried, and smiled with his broken teeth. 'Except, of course, some we will take for expenses.'

'Meanwhile,' Quince yelled, helping himself to a chicken leg. 'Let's party. I feel like we deserve a break. Tomorrow I'll be heading home with my prisoner.'

'*Gringo*,' Parra shouted above the din. 'I weesh you luck. Go with God.'

# ELEVEN

'Luther, how long we gawn be hangin' around along this durn river for?' Abel Scutt took off his battered derby hat and scratched at the lice in his matted hair. 'We ain't seen a soul in days.'

Luther Sargent sat his horse and gazed across the Rio Grande. He watched a pair of hawks, one hovering scaring a jack-rabbit into a fast twenty miles-an-hour run back towards its hole, the second waiting and pouncing from a thorn bush. There was a squeal of pain and it was all over. The hawks shared their meal. It was not a sight you often saw. Hawks usually hunted alone.

'That's what we got to do,' he gritted out. 'Wait. Be ready to pounce. I got the feelin' them double-crossing skunks who killed my men and stole my gold will be back this way to cross the river again.'

'Yes, but when will that be, Luther? Next century? Cain't you give us a few dollars on account so we an' my brothers kin go paint Brownsville red?'

'Yeah, they'll rename it Redsville after we've had our way.' Abel's brother, Jed, gave a whoop. 'I sure am tired of hangin' around like this.'

'Listen, you gutter trash, and listen good. You'll

get paid when I say so, even if we have to wait here another year.' Luther Sargent sat motionless, hawk-like himself, in his ragged chaps, sun-bleached boots, and faded shirt. Only a twitch of his moustachios expressed any feeling on his weatherbeaten face. 'I'm a man of the feud,' he growled.

'Aw, come on, Luther,' Abel whined. 'Give us a break.' He was the only one who had been with the arms-dealer when his deal had gone disastrously wrong. 'You gambled and lost. It's time to try somethang else. I got me a bank-robbin' itch.'

'Shut up, you brainless fool.' Luther deigned to glance around at Scutt, his two brothers, Jed and Ebediah, and the other couple of fleabitten gallows birds he had recruited. 'And you others, keep your weapons oiled. You booze-hoistin' deadbeats better be ready to do what I tell you and do it fast.'

'You ain't got no right to talk to us that way, Luther. Lawk's sake, you ain' payin' us much.'

'Look!' Abel gave a whistle of awe and got to his feet. 'Ain' that one of them who robbed us over there?'

'I seen him.' Luther's keen eyes had picked out the long-haired rider in black leather who had emerged on the far bank on his black horse. 'It looks like his wrists are tied.'

'Them others got him prisoner,' Abel peered across at the Texan cowboy who rode behind him, accompanied by a girl and a more wealthy-looking man fitted out in riding britches and a Panama hat. He had a long-barrelled revolver, flashing gold and diamonds, in his hand. 'We gonna take him from these three birds?'

'Whadda ye think? Cock your guns, you crab lice.'

'Hey, you see that gun that one's got? Weren't that hoity-toity Mex, Don Luis, carryin' that?'

'That's right,' Luther gritted out. 'That's gonna be mine to compensate me for my loss.'

He was not only referring to the gold and silver lost on the deal, but his right hand, his bones cracked by the black rider's bullet, and which, in its dirty bandage, rested on one knee, useless to him now. Hatred burned through him as he watched the foursome swim their ponies across the border. He was tempted to shoot them from their saddles midstream, but he wanted to hear what they had to say.

'Let 'em come,' he muttered.

As Quince, Lance and the other two, struggled their horses up the bank of the American side, Luther and his men came out of their hiding place beneath some willow boughs and confronted them. 'Hold it right there,' Luther shouted. 'I got an argument with you.'

'Aw, shee-it!' Lance hauled Beater in, startled. 'I told you not to cross here. This is the bastard Don Luis stole them guns from.'

'Yeah, and you're the bastard who ruined my hand and saved his skin, aincha?' The gun-runner doffed his bandaged hand, but held his Smith & Wesson trained on them with his left grip. 'Lucky fer me I'm ambidextrous, ain't it? You're gonna die.'

'Don Luis is dead,' the lawyer said. 'The guns are in the hands of Parra now. We will gladly pay you for your loss. We have no argument with you.'

'All right, mister, first thangs first – cough up the cash.'

'We don't have it with us, but if your return with me to San Antonio I will present you with a banker's draft. I am Modesto's right-hand man. We have no wish to upset you. We would like to do business again in the future. It was unfortunate that Arroyo jumped you, but it was no fault of ours.'

'Yeah? But it was plenty fault of *him*.' He glowered in his vicious, hawklike way at Silverlight. 'Cut him free. Give him his pistol. This is between me and him.'

'He's my prisoner,' Quince butted in, his chin set, doggedly. 'I've given my word to take him back alive. He'll get a fair trial.'

'Stay out of this, sonny. There'll be bounty on him. It'll go some way to what I'm owed.' Luther brandished the S. & W. at Rojas and Teresa. 'You two back off. I'll take you to San Antonio. We'll keep the girl hostage until the money's paid. Untie him, boy.'

'I cain't do that,' Quince murmured.

'That double-crossin' massacre weren't nuthin' to do with me,' Lance said. 'I was along under sufferance. You'll get your cash back so why not let us all pass?'

'Don't try to crowbait me, you snake in the grass. I got this ruined hand to remember *you* by. You gonna fight or not?'

'Aw, it wouldn't be fair. I got no circulation in my hands. My wrists've been tied tight for hours. Come on, I was only doing what I was paid to do. Let's forget this.'

'Forget. How can I forget? You gonna untie him, boy?' Luther growled at Quince. 'Or do you want to take his place?'

'Maybe I will.' The ageing Luther looked as iron-nerved a man who had ever levelled a gun at a stranger, but Quince was tired of being brow-beaten. 'What's the distance? Twenty paces?'

'Don't be an idjit, Quince. You ain't got a chance. Cut me free.'

'You're my prisoner and I'm taking you back.' Quince glanced at the five prairie rats who had aligned themselves behind Luther Sargent. He was not at all sure he could come out of this alive. But his word was his word. He started backing Feathers away. 'Let's get on with it.'

'Right,' Luther whispered, sitting his horse and returning his revolver to his leg holster. ''You've asked for it, boy.'

'Not so much of the boy,' Quince muttered, steadying the paint about twenty feet away. 'I'm plenty old enough to fight.' He braced himself, right arm outstretched, fingers open and ready to go for his Colt, waiting for Luther to make the first move. Maybe, he thought, these would be his last few moments on God's earth and, bitterly, the memory of Marie's scornful eyes flashed into his mind....

Even with his left Luther Sargent was fast. Forty years of frontier fighting had turned him into a kind of automaton. The S. & W. seemed to spring into his hand and was crashing out flame and deadly lead before Quince had even got his Colt out. But Quince was in luck. At that very moment Feathers, irritated by some fly, pranced and the bullet scorched past harmlessly.

*Ker-ash*! Quince's .45 boomed and, at the same time, Aristide Rojas fired the thousand-dollar revolver he had been holding clear of the water. He was aiming at Abel Scutt, who went spinning from his bronc. Horses whinnied and jumped with fear as Scutt's brothers replied with their guns. The two other gutter trash joined in. Complete bedlam reigned as Luther tried to put his third bullet into Lance, who ducked for cover beneath Beater's neck.

As suddenly, there was silence. When the gunsmoke cleared, drifting away across the river Luther Sargent was seen to be still sitting his horse like an implacable statue. Then he slowly toppled into the dust. He lay there as blood spread across his canvas shirt front. 'Aw, hell,' he groaned. 'Taken out by a kid.'

'Is he dead?' Teresa asked, as he fell back.

'Well, he ain't gonna git any older,' Silverlight drawled, and nodded at the Scutts sprawled where they had fallen. 'Neither are they.'

'It is terrible,' Teresa whispered. 'How many did you kill?'

'I don't know,' Rojas replied, matter-of-factly. 'Quince got Sargent with his first shot, but the old guy kept on shooting. I took out those three. Lucky for us they were not crackshots. Quince put down the other two. It was them or us, Teresa. It was like killing mad dogs.'

The girl shook her head. 'Holy Mary, I never thought to see you a killer.'

'We have to fight, Teresa.' Rojas held out his hand to squeeze hers. 'It is the only way.'

'You're lucky to be alive, darlin',' Lance remarked. 'Me, too. Luther can burn in hell for all I care.'

'Come on,' Quince urged them. 'Let's get out of here.'

'Agh, come on, ole buddy,' Lance wheedled. 'Cut me free. You can let me go now. I'll skip Texas. You'll never see me again. Be a pal.'

Quince grinned at him. 'If I'd let you take on Luther, and you'd beat him, I'm pretty sure I'd have been the next one on your list. So, come on, Lance, cut the crap. Let's move it.'

'I nevuh knew you were such a pig-headed sonuvabitch,' Lance sighed, but spurred his horse northwards and called back, 'Don' worry, it ain't a bad trait for a Texan.'

A hot wind hit them and the sky darkened as great blue and black clouds blew in from the Gulf of Mexico. And suddenly the rains sheeted down with the force of a hurricane. Lightning cracked along the rim of the plain and thunder boomed in their ears like a big bass drum. But the small party plodded on.

Quince had slung his slicker around his shoulders. He'd taken a pair of tight buckskin *chaparerras*, fastened down the sides with silver buckles, from one of the dead back at Don Luis's hacienda – for his blue jeans had been torn to shreds by the chaparral – and they acted as a good rain-shedder. The water poured from the brim of his hat and he tied his blue polka-dot bandanna tighter to try to stop it trickling down his back. But he bore the damp discomfort with fortitude, for all Texans regarded rain, of any sort, as a blessing. The ground would green over and the cows would put on weight and life would return.

Maybe he couldn't read or write, but Quince had been schooled in this vast wilderness of sky and space. He knew horses; he knew the pests that affected cattle; he knew how to fish and when the wild duck flew south and there was food in the sky. He spoke the Spanish lingo, and some Comanche, too. He could build a fire out of a handful of dry sagebrush. He knew the ways of the wilderness. And now he knew the scorpion-like talent of badmen, human killers, and had learned to kill them, too. He had, at the age of nineteen, learned how to survive. Although it had not occurred to him as such, young Quince, although he had yet to know a woman, in the Biblical sense, had become a man.

When they reached Three Rivers, the storm had abated to a steady downpour. He lodged his prisoner in the local jail. 'Gee,' the sheriff drawled, 'I didn't recognize you, Quince. You look like you been through it, boy. I'll send a man out to the Durhams to let 'em know you're back.'

Quince bade farewell to Rojas and Teresa who were going on to San Antonio by stage, had a bath and a shave, a meal at a local restaurant, and wandered back to the jailhouse as the Durham boys rode in.

'Well, well, lookee who's here.' Bull Durham beamed through the bars at Lance Silverlight, rolling his words with satisfaction. 'A li'l bird all ready and waitin' to have his neck stretched.'

'Howdy, Bull,' Silverlight drawled. 'Long time no see.'

'Yeah, we've come to take you on a little trip – into eternity, you might say. You'll be gittin' your reward money, Quince. We sure appreciate your co-operation, Sheriff. We know you cain't legally hang this man yourself, so we'll just take him off your hands, no questions asked.'

'Sure, Bull. Nobody's gonna mourn the demise of a lousy horse-thief. Where you gonna do it?'

'Thought we'd take him along the crik for a coupla miles where there's that big ole cottonwood. Ideal spot for a hanging.'

'Hey,' Quince interjected. 'I thought, at least, he was goin' to get a trial first.'

'Grow up, Quince,' Bull growled. 'You livin' in cloud-cuckoo-land? This rat stole sixty of our horses. He don't deserve no trial.'

'Well, I know he's guilty as hell, but—'

'Come *on*. The sooner we git rid of this stinkin' polecat the better it'll be, OK?'

'What about Mr Durham. Does he know about this?'

'The Old Man's outa town. He's gawn down to Orange Grove to pick up Marie. We'd best git this done 'fore she gits back. The Old Man'll be glad to hear he's swung. Silverlight's bin nuthin' but a pain in the ass to us.'

'Don't worry about it, Quince.' Silverlight pulled on his black gloves. 'I guess my time's come. There ain't nuthin' you or I can do about it. So long, ole buddy. How do I look? I wanna go in style. Lead on, boys.'

'Yeah.' The sheriff watched them mount up and go jogging away through the mud. 'Go boys. You're on a good undertaking.'

Bull and his brother, accompanied by several of

their range men, led the party out of town and headed away along the bank of the flooded Neuces River. They soon reached the big tree. Jack Durham sent a rope over one of its stout arms, attaching its end to a spur. The other he fashioned into a noose and slipped over the head of Lance Silverlight.

'I ain't nevuh been hung before,' Lance said, 'so just give me a coupla minutes, will ya? First, I got a few dollars left in my boot, so it's yours, Bull, if you make this hanging quick. Second, Quince, we were pals once so would you see I get a good burial and write to my mother, tell her what's happened, say I was thinkin' of her in spite of her whorin' ways?'

'I'll do that, Lance,' Quince sat his horse among the circle of other solemn cowpokes.

'OK,' Lance said. 'Let's git on with it.'

He took a deep breath and took a last look at the world as Bull intoned, 'We all agreed that by the old law of the West this thieving hoss-rustler should be hanged by his neck 'til he's dead? If any do not, speak out.'

'Yeah, me,' Quince muttered. 'He should have a trial.'

'You're outvoted,' Bull said, as the other punchers made no comment. 'OK?'

'Ain't you gonna say a few words from the Bible?' Lance asked.

'How do I know Bible words? You'll be wantin' me to send for the preacher next.'

'Come on, git on with it,' Jack shouted, and stepped forward to whack Beater across the hindquarters. The horse leapt forwards and Lance was jerked from the saddle to hang from the rope, his legs kicking, frenziedly.

Old Man Durham was driving his buggy along the precipitous trail that followed the course of the Neuces valley towards his ranch, his daughter Marie by his side.

'What's going on down there?' he asked.

'Oh, my God.' Marie clapped her hand to her mouth. 'It's Lance. I'd recognize them dark glasses anywhere.'

'Hellfire and damnation. They can't do that. I ain't given the say-so.' Durham hauled the rig to a halt, grabbed his rifle and yelled down to the men. 'Wait!' But nobody seemed to hear him as Silverlight was launched into space, swinging back and forth. Durham, without hesitation, squinted along his sights, and fired. Lance hit the deck hard as the rope was severed.

'Just in the nick of time to save him from Old Nick. Let's go see if he's still in the land of the living.'

'Pa,' Bull bellowed. 'What you doing? I thought you wanted him dead.'

'Don't be a dang fool.' The Old Man beckoned his sons to one side and said in a lowered voice, 'Your sister's pregnant. You think I'm gonna hang my grandson's father? You want the kid to live with that for the rest of his life?'

'Pregnant?' Bull gulped his surprise. 'You mean she's got a babby in her belly?'

'Don't tell the whole world,' Durham muttered.

Marie was down on her knees hugging Lance to her as he rubbed at his rope-burned throat. 'Where am I?' he asked. 'In heaven with the angels? Is that you, Marie? How'd yo git here?'

'You're alive, my darlin',' she cried, kissing him.

'Git on your feet, you varmint.' John Durham poked him with the rifle. 'Your wanderin' days are over. We're gonna go find a preacher. You *want* to marry her, don't you?'

'Well, if you put it like that.' Lance grinned. 'Course I do. That is, if my pal Quince, here, can be best man.'

'Welcome to the family, you sidewinder.' Durham offered his hand. 'Maybe I'll buy you a little spread along Atacosa way. Far enough away so I don't have to have nuthin' to do with you, but near enough so I git to see my grandkids. OK?'

'Thanks, Dad.' Lance looked at the glowering Durham brothers as he removed the noose from his neck. 'Nice to have you as in-laws, boys. No hard feelings, I hope?'

Reluctantly they shook his proffered hand. 'I cain't say I'm happy about this,' Bull said. 'I fancied them dollars in your boot.' He burst out laughing and punched Lance, playfully, in the gut. 'You durn lucky sonuvagun. I came within a second of gittin' 'em.'

'Yuh,' Silverlight croaked out. 'I figured you was givin' the slow burn. Otherwise I'da been dead and gawn.'

# TWELVE

It was not exactly a shotgun wedding, more a Winchester one. Nudging Silverlight with the business end of his rifle, Old Man Durham pushed Marie into the little white-washed chapel at Three Rivers. 'No, we ain't got time for you to git fancied up, Daughter. We need to git this done.'

'But what about a ring?' Marie asked.

'You can use my wedding ring 'til we got time to buy you another.'

One of the boys had gone to rustle up the preacher and, when he arrived, the Old Man bawled, 'Let's git on with the ceremony.' He poked Lance with the rifle. '*You*! Git up closer. I wanna keep an eye on you.'

The ring was much too large but, at least, it was a ring, Marie thought, and sighed with relief after the 'I do's' and Lance warmly kissed her. Her weeks of heartache and worry were over.

The cowpokes had sat their mokes outside in the rain, guns at the ready, to make sure Silverlight didn't try to make a break for freedom. John

Durham treated them all to a festive supper in the town saloon, and proposed a toast to the happy couple.

'Now,' he said, a tad worried, 'we got to go break the news to your mother. C'm on. We'll head back to the ranch.'

They tumbled out on to the sidewalk, laughing and joking, when suddenly two men came galloping down the street. They spun their horses to a halt in a spray of mud outside the saloon, and one of them, the acne-faced Jesse Bolton, had his revolver in an outstretched arm aiming at Lance Silverlight. 'Time to face the hatchet,' he cried. 'Die, you dog.'

Lance had had his Lightning returned to him but he had time only to half-draw it from its holster as the bullet crashed into his chest, knocking him back against the saloon wall. 'What—?' was all he could say as he slid down.

Quince Simms threw himself in front of Marie as the other rider fired, too. The bullet scorched his cheek, but he had his .45 out and his reply catapulted the would-be assassin from his horse. He watched with horror as he writhed in the mud.

Before Jesse Bolton could aim a second shot, John Durham had levered his rifle, with the rapid instinct of an infantryman, and put a bullet between his eyes. They watched him topple over and croak his last.

Marie was down on her knees sobbing over Lance. 'Why?' she cried. 'Why?'

Lance was struggling to live and coughed out his words. 'I kilt two of their kin. Them sorta rats don't forget. Let's hope it's over now.'

'Darling,' Marie said, 'you're going to be all right.'

'No, I ain't. I'm goin' fast.' Lance beckoned the wrangler to him. 'Quince, ole pal, look after Marie for me, look after my child. You're a good man. Don't let him make the mistakes I done.'

Quince knelt beside him and gripped his hand. 'I'll do what I can, Lance.'

'Thanks.' Lance tried for the last time to force a reckless smile. 'I bequeath you my sun specs. I know you allus fancied 'em.' With his dying strength he pressed Marie's and Quince's hands together with his. 'This is the guy you shoulda married, Marie. He's crazy 'bout ya.'

His head fell back and he was gone. Quince took the sun specs from him and closed his cold blue eyes. 'He weren't all bad,' he said. 'Just wild.'

They crossed Lance's arms across his chest and, as they still knelt beside him, the girl intertwined her fingers into those of Quince. 'Is it true what he said?'

'I guess it is.' The wrangler met her blue eyes. 'First time I saw you, you burned your brand into me, Marie. Seems like I'm branded for life.'

John Durham was standing over them, listening. 'Hey, go fetch that preacher,' he called. 'My gal's too young to be a widow woman. Tell him we're gonna have another wedding. An' I better go git Olga for this one. It ain't something she'd want to miss.'

He went outside, clambered on his horse, then pointed a finger at Quince. 'And you! I'm booking you into the hotel tonight. You got one night of wedded bliss. But you'll have to be back at the ranch by daylight. We got some catchin' up to do. We're movin' them dogies north.'

'Yee-hah!' Bull bellowed. 'Kansas here we come. Dodge City you better be ready fer us.'

'Yeah, I wouldn't miss it.' Quince stood with his arm around Marie and smiled at her. 'But, honey, I'll be back for you.'

# AFTERWORD

So, while Texans prospered in freedom, it would be another thirty years before Mexicans gained their liberty. Ignacio Parra was eventually shot from the saddle when he tried to rob a heavily guarded silver mine payroll. But his young lieutenant, Pancho Villa, fought on to finally ride into Mexico City with his conquering revolutionaries. The dictatorship of Diaz collapsed like a pack of cards and he scuttled for safety in exile. A new president, Madero, was installed. But he, like Villa, was later assassinated in a hail of bullets.